SUNLIT

SHORT STORIES

IVAN FERNANDEZ

Ivan Fernandez

SUNLIT

Contents

v

Preface

My earliest serious attempts at laying it out on the page – some time in my late teens – resulted in a few verses in the style of haiku, some more conventional rhymed and free verse (also relatively short), and one short story. My first paid gig – while at university – was as a freelance copywriter, where again, the constant refrain was "less is more".

When it comes down to writing... any writing (a letter or email to a family member or a research report at work), I tend to prefer concentration of expression over elaborate narrative. Even my first published book – *How Art Can Change Your Life: Life Lessons from Artists Past and Present* – was a collection of brief chapters on largely self-contained themes.

My reading life, on the other hand, has taken in both the short form and the epic (how can you not have time for the depth and breadth of thought and feeling in Dostoevsky's *The Brothers Karamazov* or Hugo's *Les Misérables*!). In truth, the 'peak experiences' of journeying through a great novel have only helped me approach short story writing with a stronger sense of connection and confidence.

But there has always been something about the story-in-one-sitting that has fascinated me. From childhood favourites

– *Aesop's Fables*, *The Arabian Nights*, *Panchatantra*, and Arthur Conan Doyle's *The Adventures of Sherlock Holmes*, through to evergreen favourites from O Henry, for example, or from that master of all short story masters, Anton Chekhov.

These, and every other great short story, promise to not keep us long, but because they are snapshots, they force us to strip away distractions and see only what deserves to be seen.

Because they are content to simply ask the questions, they force us to find the answers or live more courageously with the questions that have no answers.

In writing some stories in this collection, I have done what every self-respecting author would do – mine freely and unapologetically from told and untold events in my own life and that of family and friends. But where inspired by actual events or people, those memories have gone through multiple reinventions to suit the purpose and pulse of the story. At times, I have also indulged in that other exasperating habit of authors – of voicing my own musings, reflections, and convictions. Here again, I offer no apology. Stories and story-telling come from the same space as lived experience and can often provide more profound insight and greater consolation than the most reliable body of facts. As we often struggle to make sense and meaning of our dark and imperfect spaces, it is sometimes, those little flecks of light that show us the way forward or the way inward.

A number of people have made this book possible, and my thanks go to them. My wife, Marion, and my children, Olivia and Raphael; for indulging me the hours that went into writing and rewriting. And my parents, brothers, sisters, nieces, and nephews; for the encouragement and support given to me every time I sent over an instalment of stories.

Ivan Fernandez
Sydney, NSW, Australia
April 2023

I

Little boy with a bat

I could hear the three boys yelling as they crowded into the garage.

"We've got him!"

The oldest boy's declaration did not betray even the slightest doubt.

I scurried between the cans of paint and hopped up the pipe that led to the top shelf. Maybe if I was fast enough...

Bang!! One of the younger boys – a couple of years younger than the oldest – smashed a tennis racquet on the pipe just centimetres away from my whiskers. Thrown with the impact, I lost hold of the pipe and plopped clumsily onto the cardboard boxes stacked high against the wall.

"Blast it!! The little devil! You almost got him!" The oldest boy growled, while the two younger ones shrieked in delight.

But this was far from funny. They'd already poisoned my only sibling who had made the mistake of trying out the rat baits under the barbeque. I found him headfirst in the grass – hind legs sticking up; motionless, cold, and hard, as only a dead rat can be.

But that victory only whipped the young ones into a frenzy. They wanted to finish the job.

Their father never parked the car in the garage, and over time it had become a cluttered dumping ground.

Now the oldest was prodding open each cardboard box with a rusty pipe which was conveniently at hand in the garage. The Federer freak was standing at the other side of the boxes ready to serve another ace if I popped up at that end. The youngest boy – still plump and unafraid – was standing guard at the garage door; just in case I made any attempt to make a run for it through their legs and out into the garden.

The oldest was doing a very meticulous job, ramming the pipe through every box. I had to make my move. There was hardly a moment to lose!

My getaway was blocked by the wall on one side and the Federer freak on the other. There was only one way out. I had to make a dash through them and get the hell out of that garage.

I darted out of the last box, dropped fast onto the floor, scampered in between the legs of the oldest boy, and made a dash for the door. "Whoa! He's getting away!!" The oldest boy swivelled and landed one blow with his rusty pipe on the floor. He missed me by a foot. I didn't bother celebrating... my eyes were fixed on the great outdoors behind the little fellow guarding the door. In a second, I had dashed across the garage in a wild zig zag line.

I was almost home. But almost is not quite it, is it?

That little fellow at the door had heaved an old, heavy cricket bat that was leaning against the door and stood perfectly still – bat raised high – waiting to strike.

I dashed to the left and hopped to the right... I was not going to let some brat drop me with his freakin bat!

Bang! His single blow broke my back and smashed my hind legs. I gasped hard and looked up at my killer. While the older boy and the Federer freak jumped and hollered in the background, this little boy looked down at my mangled body with quiet interest. My head and front legs twitched furiously... uncontrollably. So, this is what it felt to be snuffed out by another being! It was humiliating... demeaning... crushing.

From where I lay, I could see the sunlit grass through the garage door. It was a lovely day. And I was so close.

The little boy took a deep breath, pushed back the mop of hair that had fallen over his sweaty brow, heaved his bat up again, lined it up just above my head and brought the willow down hard... and fast.

2

Before the family holiday

**2:30 pm... in the tow truck with the tow truck driver;
the smashed up 8-seater in tow**

Did he lose it with you?

No, no... he was pretty decent. Just said that it was a brand-new Lexus.

Ouch!

Yes... I know... it must hurt.

Looks like he will be sans Lexus for a while.

His insurance will cover it.

You mean, your insurance will cover it.

Yes... agree.

But how much will you be out of pocket?

Don't know... maybe two thousand.

You are not having a good day... are you?

My brakes did not hold.

Okay... so there was a problem with the brakes.

I'm serious... there was a problem with the brakes.

Mate... that's what they always say –

"The brakes didn't hold".

I swear.

But you are down two thousand and he is without his Lexus.

Yes.

Okay mate... I believe you. Not trying to make it worse than it is, but you will also be docked for this tow job.

How much?

Two fifty.

Okay.

Just put your feet up when you get home, have a beer, and be thankful you are still alive... and that you did not put anybody in hospital or the morgue today.

You take card?

Yes.

7:00 pm... returning from the airport after picking up my brother's family

You've lost weight.

Really? That's nice to know.

How long has it been?

Three years.

Seems longer. It's so good to see you.

Yes... same here.

Gosh... we are so looking forward to this.

Uncle, are we doing the Opera House?

Of course, that's day one.

Yey! And what's day two?

Day two is down south to Pebbly beach.

Yes!! Is that where we can get up close with the kangaroos?

Yes.

And Day three?

That's a surprise.

I love surprises!

I know you do.

Son, sit back.

Okay Dad.

I thought you'd bring the 8-seater that you were going to hire out for the week.

You know what... I did start the afternoon off with the 8-seater from the rental. But I rear-ended someone just when I was two minutes from home.

What!

Yes. Something wrong with the brakes.

Did you get hurt?

No, nothing. Just pretty shaken. You know for a moment there I thought that this was the end.

That bad, eh?

Yes, I couldn't slow down enough. The 8-seater had to be towed off.

You should have told me... we'd have taken a cab from the airport.

No... I'm fine now.

And how much is that going to set you back by?

Don't have the exact figure yet... the insurance company will call back tomorrow.

And what did you rear-end?

A Lexus.

Wow! And the driver? Is he okay?

Yes... he's fine. But it must have been a shock for him as well.

What did he say when he got out?

Nothing... he was pretty decent. Just said that it was a brand-new Lexus.

3

Down a sloping road

It all unfolded in slow motion.

Pedalling furiously, the young boy was exhilarated at the new found freedom of cycling without supervision for the first time.

Something had clicked and he was no longer a wobbling wreck trying to stay in balance.

With each passing second, as he gained speed, he felt a high like he had not known in a while.

But there was no time to pause. There were decisions to be made. He was nearing the end of the little lane. If he turned right, he would be onto the main road and a lot more traffic to contend with. If he turned left, no traffic, but the road sloped down.

Traffic or a steep sloping road?

He turned left.

As he felt the road giving way under him, he realised that he did not have to pedal anymore.

He laughed heartily.

This was too good.

But as he zipped effortlessly down, he sensed his bicycle gathering even more speed.

Scanning ahead to what was seemed like the end of the road – where the slope plateaued – he saw an elderly couple shuffling slowly as they started to cross the road. Really slowly.

The problem was the old man.

Not just old.

He looked ill. And he only appeared to stay upright with the aid of his wife who carefully steered him forward.

Resting his weight unashamedly on her steady out-stretched hand, he bowed his head as he willed himself into the next step.

It hit the young boy suddenly. The old couple were not going to make it across the road before his cycle passed. But he was coming in too fast. And in that moment, the last thing to occur to him was to apply the brakes or to swerve away. He couldn't. He had gambled on making it safely down the sloping road. But he had not factored in the complication of an old and feeble couple crossing the road at that time.

In that blurred slow motion of an impending crash, he knew that his cycle would hit the old woman first.

But when he was but a few yards from impact, the old man spotted him.

In a second, he had straightened up and pushed his wife behind him. His eyes widening, stretching out his thin arms, he grabbed the handlebar and brought the lurching cycle and boy to an instant halt.

The boy fell off with the jolt, but did not hurt himself. The old man held onto the cycle and looked on as the boy picked himself sheepishly off the ground.

He mumbled a brief apology, got back on, and pedalled away as fast as he could.

Just before he turned the road, he looked back.

The sudden exertion had drained the very life out of the old man. He bowed down again as his wife quickly regained her composure and steadied him across the road.

4

The end

She was alone when she passed.

I am truly sorry, Ken. It must be difficult for you.

I'm not talking about me, Mary.

I know.

I promised her.

What?

I promised her I'd be there for her.

But you were. All these years. Every setback. Every trip to the hospital. Every hour that she remained lucid.

You know, Mary, this world... it's not Eden.

I know.

The ones who are feeble are not spared.

I know.

We are just unthinking pawns.

Ken, you must move forward.

We are no masters of our fate.

You must find a way out of this.

We are broken.

Ken... really!

Born broken.

Did your son and family visit this week?

No, I haven't seen them since the funeral.

They will come... I'll give them a call.

No, don't Mary. Let them come when they come.

Okay Ken, whatever you say.

He must be hitting his mid-forties? Your son?

Forty-six this August.

Time flies.

Yes. It was only the other day when I lost him for a full five minutes at the Easter Show.

Five minutes? The Easter Show?

The Royal Easter Show. He was seven. My daughter was five. They had come out the other side of the Spinning Coaster. And I was waiting up the front. My son... he just started walking into the crowds, calling for me.

Those are massive crowds, Ken. Anyone can get lost in that!

Yes. I knew I only had a few minutes before he got completely out of reach.

What did you do?

I ran... you know, in a zig zag kind of way... fanning out from where he had got off the ride. Shouting out his name.

And?

People looked at me like I had gone mad.

It must have been agony for you.

Yes, but I found him, Mary.

Of course you did.

He was still walking through the crowds... sobbing quietly. I spotted him from behind... rushed up and gathered him in my arms.

Oh Ken. He will never forget that Easter Show.

I know I haven't.

5

Fragments... in bed

What are you thinking of?
Nothing.
Tell me, what are you thinking of?
Nothing in particular, Jess.
You can't be thinking of nothing!
Okay, I can't be thinking of nothing.
Then tell me.
What?
What are you thinking of?

6

So how well do you know your classical music?

Mum, I had a terrible dream.

What was it, Seb?

I dreamt that we were all held hostage by a gunman at home.

Why would you have such a scary dream?

It's a dream, Mum!

Okay... so what happened in this dream?

There was this guy who had you, Daddy, and Sid tied up in chairs in the living room.

And where were you?

Right there... but in front of the turntable.

Doing what?

Saving your lives!

How Seb?

This gunman... this freak... he kept saying to me in a sickening drawl – "So how well do you know your classical music, son?"

What?

"How well do you know your classical music, son?"

Okay... and then what?

He said, "You're going to stand with your back to me. And I'm going to pick up LPs from this fascinating collection that your dad has here." And I said, "Please, Mister... please let them go." And he said, "Not so fast, not so fast. Let's test your classical music IQ!" And I said, "Please Sir, we won't tell anybody... just leave us." And he said, "No clues... no multiple choice. I just play a piece at random... and you've got to name the composer and the work. Get it right, and I untie one of them. Get it wrong, and I shoot." "No Mister... please." But he wouldn't listen. I could hear him fumbling as he took an LP out of its sleeve. "Ah... no peeking, boy!!" "No Sir, I'm not."

And why Seb, were we not calling out for help?

He had the three of you bound and gagged, Mum!

Okay... carry on.

I heard the stylus drop onto the LP. And I heard him shove the gun at Daddy's head. The LP crackled. Brahms *First Symphony*, first movement. Too easy!! I blurted out after the first few seconds: "That's Brahms *First Symphony*, first movement." He stopped the turntable. Silence. I think he was checking the album cover to make sure I had it right. "Oooh now, so we have a classical music expert here, I see!" he drawled. "Good on you, kiddo! You've just saved your dad's life! Let's see how you do with this next." And with that he pulled out another LP, put it on, and shoved the gun at your head, Mum.

Mine! And what happened, Seb?

It was the Beethoven *Emperor Concerto*, first movement, Mum! This guy had no idea that I actually listened to classical music!

So, you saved me, Seb! How sweet!

Yes Mum. I did.

Okay, what happened after? This is getting nerve-wracking. How did you do with Sid's turn?

It was bloody Stravinsky Mum...how was I to know which piece!

What! He killed Sid in your dream!!!

No, Mum. I blurted out, "Its Stravinsky... its Stravinsky... but please Mister, I don't know which piece of Stravinsky's." "Sorry, boy, that's only a half-right answer... so your little brother will take it in the leg then." And bang! He shot Sid in the leg.

Morning Mum, morning Seb... what's this all about?

Nothing Sid, sit down and have your cereal. Your brother here should really pay more attention to the 20th century composers, I think.

7

Last customer for the day

It was nearing the end of school holidays and I was just finishing off with a schoolboy – straightforward crew cut; no styling, no fuss.

Old Mr Bashir walked in at 4 pm.

Our hair salon was not very busy that day, so I had told the other guy to take off early while I tackled the schoolboy, and then I'd only have Mr Bashir.

"Afternoon Mr Bashir... it's good to see you."

"Afternoon Herb. Lovely, sunny afternoon!"

"Be with you in a couple of minutes."

"No rush Herb... it's not like I've got places to go to."

The old man settled in to wait.

Mr Bashir was in his mid-eighties. His wife had died last year and he seemed to be struggling with life as a widower. He lived a few minutes' walk from the main drag in our suburb – in a one-bedroom ground floor apartment. No relatives to speak of, except a daughter and her family overseas, who he only saw every other year.

We'd see him often as he walked slowly past the shops; a kind but vacant look on his face. At times he really did go in to pick up a few frozen meals to stock up his freezer, but most times he walked the main drag just to walk.

"Come on over Mr Bashir", I said beckoning him to the chair vacated by the surly schoolboy who slinked out after paying.

"I haven't seen you for a while Mr Bashir... must be three months?"

"Yes Herb... I don't like missing my haircut every second month. But I've been a bit under the weather these last few weeks."

"All good now Mr Bashir?"

"Yes, I'm through with a course of antibiotics... much better now, thank you, Herb."

Mr Bashir settled into the chair. I swung a fresh cape around him. He closed his eyes, sunk lower in the chair, and let out a weary but contented sigh.

I knew the drill for the old man. No-frills, classic side part. Short, but not too short. No shears... no razor... just scissors... and certainly no squirts of water on the head (Mr Bashir held onto a lifelong belief that hair left wet gave him a cold).

Customers to the salon are easily bracketed into one of two camps – the nodders – who promptly doze off the moment you apply comb and scissors – and those who don't. Mr Bashir did not snooze when I got going, but his eyes closed, and he looked so gratified the moment I started that it was a shame to disturb his reverie with small talk.

So I worked in a calm, comfortable silence.

This time, as he got off the chair and paid, he seemed particularly introspective. At the door, he stopped, turned around and said: "You know Herb, that's the first time someone has actually touched me in three months. That haircut reminded me of my dear mother who used to stroke my head so I could drift off to sleep at night. Funny thing for someone my age to say, but maybe when you reach this far, you are allowed the luxury of feeling like a child again... You take care, Herb."

He shuffled out and I cleaned up before shuttering down for the day.

8

3:03 pm

2:55 pm.

The last of the TV ads wrap up. They've finished with prize money talk. They've zoomed in on the best of the day's fashion on display off the track at Flemington. They've run through the list of horses, jockeys, trainers, owners, and odds. They've dissected every possible scenario with Melbourne's fickle weather. They've sung the national anthem. The horses reach the starting barriers.

Three more left to load.

They are all in now.

It's gotten quite noisy across all three tables that we've taken at the pub close to our office on Pitt Street. I quickly scan my picks in the office sweepstakes.

Southern Symphony, Prince of New Holland, Primary, and *Amadeus.*

Four picks in a draw of 24 horses (down to 21 now, after

three late scratchings). Ten dollars a pick. First place wins 60% of the total prize, second place 30%, and third place 10%.

Will – seated to my left – peeks at my list. "Wow!! Terence, you have two of the favourites in your list!!"

Kim – seated across – chimes in, "Terence is always so damn lucky at this." Then turning to her neighbour, Oscar, she continues, "You know Oscar, I might as well fill you in – you being the new guy and all. The resident racing meister over there wins every year at the sweepstakes. Don't ask me how. But thought I'd let you know... just in case you had notions of making it big today."

Oscar stares across the table with mock hostility. "So how do you do it, Terence?"

"I don't DO anything, Oscar! It's a straightforward lucky draw from the hat."

Geoff – from across the next table – is holding forth on the obscene amounts of money that the country puts into bets for this one race. Zora is recounting to her friend where she was the time *Makybe Diva* completed the unprecedented three-in-a-row win in 2005.

Will goes into all the weird and wonderful new betting options he's tried apart from win bet, place bet, each way bet, and the trifecta.

Lots of animated discussion around the three surprise last-minute scratchings – especially from Diny and Tim's corner – dismayed that their picks are no longer in the race.

I glance at my list again – *Southern Symphony*, *Prince of New Holland*, *Primary*, and *Amadeus*. None from my picks amongst the scratchings.

It's almost as if I'm willing them – trainers, owners, jockeys, and horses to do it for me... again.

No foul weather to delay the start.

3.00 pm
The field is set for "the race that stops the nation".

Standby... and... they're off!

Undertone and *Exuberant* are away on the inside. *Ninja Trooper* shares the front with *Contender*. They've put two lengths between them and *Emissary*. *Southern Symphony* is out wide. Further back is *Primary*.

A length and a half, and there's *Xanadu*. That's where they are tightly packed. Poking through the middle is *Amadeus*. He's settled nicely. Behind him *Spirited Pilgrim*, *Dark Emperor*, *Statesman*, *Wind Walker*, and *First Savant*. Right at the end of the field is local hope – *Wild Wraith*, alongside *Scheherazade*, *Giselle*, *Brimstone*, *Pollock*, and *DiDonato*.

They leave the straight.

Will, Kim and Zora start hopping about as if it's the homestretch. They get shut down immediately.

On the fence is *Prince of New Holland*.

Southern Symphony stays wide.

And *Contender* breaks out to take up the lead. *Exuberant* second and *Undertone* third.

1,800 left to go. And *Amadeus* has taken up the lead... *Southern Symphony* in second, and *Xanadu* third.

Amadeus backer, Geoff starts hollering in glee.

Trying to slot in on the outside is *First Savant*.

Tucked away on the inside is *Dark Emperor*.

Wild Wraith is coming over.

1,100 left to go.

In the lead now – *Southern Symphony*, *First Savant* second, *Dark Emperor* third, and *Prince of New Holland* fourth.

Starting to gain ground on the outside is *Xanadu*.

Still well back – *Scheherazade*, *Giselle*, *Brimstone*, *Pollock* and *DiDonato*. No change there.

Diny curses freely. Apart from his one scratched entry, he's stuck with *DiDonato* and *Giselle* – both reluctant to break out from the back.

Movement in the front... *Dark Emperor* takes the lead!

Getting closer to the pack in front is *Amadeus* who had dropped back for a bit.

Right behind, *Xanadu*.

As they run the turn, *DiDonato* drops away completely and is out of the race! Not sure what happened there.

But now, poised to surge ahead at the front is *First Savant*!

Coming to the turning at the 700.

In the middle, *Undertone* is looking for a way between *Contender* and *Exuberant*.

Approaching the 400 metres.

Prince of New Holland takes the lead.

Amadeus is about to go.

Sneaking up behind is *Undertone*.

They come down the straight.

200 metres to go!

Prince of New Holland neck and neck with *Amadeus*!!

This is going to get down to the wire.

The sporadic cheering now steadies into a sustained roar from all our tables. Lots of fist-pumping and hopping about.

At the 100!

Here comes *Undertone* on the outside. Jockey Rene Riggs digging in for this last 100 metres.

Kim is ecstatic. *Undertone* is one of her picks.

And then suddenly... from the outside, *Southern Symphony* makes a late and unexpected charge for the finish.

I'm shouting and stomping. Kim is screaming hysterically. Zora knocks over her drink.

3:03 pm

3,200 metres done.

Southern Symphony has just pulled off a brilliant, breath-taking, last-minute win.

And I've – not unexpectedly – won the first prize at the office sweepstakes... again!

"That's voodoo, man!" Oscar looks at me in awe.

"That's so unfair!" Kim barely contains her disappointment.

Rachel's text message comes promptly after the race.

"How much?" she asks.

"I had *Southern Symphony*." I reply.

"You lucky devil!!"

As we finish drinks, I hear rumblings from the next table – "This is fixed! How can he win every year!!"

I smile, shrug, and make a mental note to buy them all some coffee and doughnuts tomorrow morning... always helps to soften the blow.

9

How could he!

Driving home after the concert

So, Joel?

What Mum?

How did you enjoy that?

Good Mum.

You don't sound very enthusiastic, Joel. What's the matter?

Nothing Mum.

You've been looking forward to this since the start of the year, right?

Uhmm.

And?

It was good Mum.

Just good, Joel? Your all-time favourite singer! WolfGang!

Yes Mum.

And the staging, the props, and the lighting... how good was that!

Good Mum.

And he sang 'Distant Home'... we thought he was not going to... but then he whipped it out as his final encore!

Yes Mum.

Oh Joel... what happened? Are you crying? What's wrong baby?

He forgot.

What Joel? What did he forget?

He forgot the words in the second verse.

Is that why you're crying?

How could he Mum?

You poor thing! I forget my own phone number on a bad day, Joel. Anyone can forget. Give him a break. He's hitting fifty this year.

He cannot forget Mum. It should have been perfect. I waited for it. It should have been perfect.

10

Declared dead

Did I tell you about the most traumatic twenty seconds of my preteen years?

I was back from school early one afternoon. They had to shut early, and Mum was still at work. So rather than hang around on campus, I decided to walk home.

I got home only to realise that without the keys, I couldn't get in till Mum came back.

It was the peak of summer, and I was not looking forward to being roasted in our front yard. So I strolled over to our neighbour's front door and knocked.

"Hello Rick, you're home early?"

"Yes Ma'am. School shut early today. Mum does not know. So can I just sit here till she's back?"

"No problem, Rick... come right in."

"Thank you, Ma'am."

"I'm finishing off some pasta in the kitchen, so why don't you go into the living... Jim should be there."

She was well into her eighties, but still alert and sprightly. Not so her husband, Jim. He was what we kids would classify as 'almost gone'.

I walked into the living room and froze.

Sprawled out on the reclining sofa was 'almost gone' Jim – eyes shut and still as a rock.

"Afternoon sir!" I ventured.

No response.

"Hullo sir." I offered.

No response.

Was he asleep?

I couldn't tell.

I took a step closer to investigate.

No snoring... no sign of even quiet breathing! And there was no question of my checking his pulse... I did not even know how to!

To my eleven-year-old brain this was all not looking good.

No blood. No sign of forced entry.

Did he just die in his sleep?

I was no expert on the subject, but he looked gone to me.

Did he have to do that just when I happened to rock by?

My head became dizzy – I could picture the story in the local newspaper the next day - Retired Lawyer, Jim Greenwood... died of natural causes. Or was it died of old age? It seemed a peaceful, painless way to go... in your sleep.

But what if his wife thought that I had something to do with it? What if they sent me to juvenile prison for the manslaughter of a harmless retiree! I should have waited on in school.

There was no time to debate next steps. With a violent start, Jim jumped up as if struck by lightning.

I let out a stifled yelp.

If walking in on a body with no sign of life was not upsetting enough, I also had to witness this back-from-the-dead moment. Jim gasped and sputtered on the sofa while I stood motionless.

"Jim... sir... I thought you were... I thought something happened!"

"It's nothing boy... I just dozed off here without my CPAP. Did I stop breathing for a while?"

Decades later, I maintain that those twenty seconds – as an unsuspecting eleven-year-old in front of an old man with sleep apnoea – was something I wouldn't wish even on my worst enemy.

But then again....

11

Failed Attempt No. 6

The white canvas looks at me.

And I look back.

I guess, I must make the first move.

I squirt some yellow ochre onto the palette and mix in some titanium white. Then I pick up a 2-inch flat brush and load some of the paint onto it. And now that I'm committed, I smack hard and fast onto the canvas.

Will it be a sunrise? No. A sunset.

Will there be water? Yes.

People? No.

Some greenery? No.

That's it... just sky, sun, and sea.

Soon ultramarine blue, crimson red, sap green and burnt umber make their way onto the canvas.

Time to add some body to the painting.

I plop some glossy gel medium onto the palette, swap the

flat brush for a palette knife and lay it on with heavy, buttery, impasto strokes.

It's coming together... I think.

More contrast here. Some highlights there.

White and cadmium yellow for the sun at its brilliant, blinding core. More subdued orange and ash grey around. Purple black clouds in the corners of the canvas - to suggest the encroaching darkness.

The sombre reflection of the sky in the waters - to hint that the day is losing something. Something that can never be relived.

I step back.

The wonderfully vivid composition on canvas now looks tight... constricted... soulless.

No hesitation.

I load black paint onto my brush and work quickly.

In under a minute, the canvas is black. Only black.

There goes the sunset.

The black canvas looks at me.
And I look back.

12

My only gripe

My name is Alec Larsen.

But I guess you would know me better as the country singer who sang, '*Thumping Good*'.

I started writing and singing songs well before I could finish school. And it took such a hold that I didn't bother with university. Fact is, I didn't bother with pretty much anything else but songs and singing. At least not for a long time.

Do you know why I'm sure there is life after death? Because now and again we are allowed – in this world of troubles – glimpses of some things that we sense are just too good for us. For me, music and music-making was that something 'just too good'. Something celestial; that, by divine providence, we foolish mortals were allowed to experience... even in our small and timid lives.

Of course, I realised very early that there was nothing inimitable about my voice – certainly no Merle Haggard or

John Denver. But as long as there was Bob Dylan, there was hope that you didn't need a great voice to cut through the clutter.

The trick was to write songs that stayed with you long after the melody had ended. Fortunately for me, that seemed to come easier than to most.

But I really did cut through the clutter only after my first Billboard hit, 'Thumping Good'. That was a full decade and a half after I'd first started singing nightclubs and pubs for a living.

I admit I was still finding my own sound in that time... believe me, it takes time! But not all of those early efforts were unremarkable.

Despite the title, 'Thumping Good' actually came from a dark place. It was a song of hope, but more a daft and defiant hope in the face of inexorable trials. The *Rolling Stone* review claimed that in 'Thumping Good' the songwriter "was onto something good. Something true. An out-of-the-blue anthem for a desperate and exhausted middle class". Whatever it was, it worked! Wide radio airplay... appearances on national TV shows... flattering covers of the song by some of the best names in country music... and best of all, a string of requests from those same stars to write songs for them.

That was over forty years ago. And in that time I moved on to songs with more nuance, more introspection, and certainly, with more personal lyrics.

Recorded six number-one country singles after 'Thumping Good', a couple of chart-topping duets, a pop crossover album that did better than the critics expected.

Toured widely.

Changed record labels and crew more than a couple of times (not surprising given that I was constantly at war with my producers, promoters, and agents!). Took my fair share of hostile reviews (I didn't mind that one bit... most critics are just half-deaf, insecure, incorrigible idiots anyway).

Had to give up playing the guitar live ten years ago (something to do with the nerves in my left hand). Lost my wife... and last year, a grandchild. Lost too many friends to count. Enjoyed an all too brief comeback a couple of years ago.

And here I am... wondering why.

Why nothing I did after 'Thumping Good' seemed good enough for them? Don't get me wrong – I'm not in one-hit-wonder territory. But you'd never have guessed that a signature song would turn into a curse on the house of Larsen. But it did become just that.

It was not only the one encore I simply had to do at every concert, it was also the only song interviewers seemed interested in talking to me about.

I wish I had a dollar for every time someone came up to me in a restaurant or bar gleefully sticking out a greasy paw as they declared, "They're playing your song, Al!"

What about 'On the brink', 'It's a Splendid Thing', 'Goodbye Champ', 'Rust in the Rain', or 'This Side of Eden'? Or even the stripped bare, 'Alone and Good'? And whatever happened to 'Chronicle of a Gambler', 'Remembrance' or 'Chockfull'? What about all those other songs I bled out of my days, that I hoped to count for something?

It's not that I am discounting all the good fortune that's come my way. It's been a great ride! It's just that when the glow fades and life's work is done, you'd hope that there is more than just one song to remember you by.

But then again, this is one script that you don't get to write.

13

Under attack

It wasn't a remarkable movie at all. In fact, the only image that kept playing back to me was that of a woman's ghost floating up from the bottom of a village well. Not recommended daily intake for unsuspecting kids, but there you have it... you cannot unsee some things in life.

It was late by the time we turned off the TV and decided to wrap up. I was to go up to the terrace to check the water level in our overhead tank. Not feeling too brave that night, I asked my younger brother, George to tag along.

Before we had got to the stairs, our eldest brother, Joseph decided that this was too good an opportunity to pass up. So with devilish intent, he snuck up to the terrace and hid behind the door connecting the stairwell to the terrace.

We had the light on in the stairway. But it was pitch black on the terrace. With George in tow, I clambered up the stairs and reached the door that opened to the terrace.

On cue, Joseph – who was hiding behind the door – jumped out from behind – his arms contorted like a demented puppet. And he threw in the obligatory noises of a demonic spirit.

To be fair to me, young kids do not generally expect Pennywise to pop out on terraces at night when you have mundane chores to do – like checking water levels in overhead tanks. It's just not within the realm of possibility.

And just to set the record straight – I had just seen visions of ghosts floating up from the damp and dark recesses of wells.

I let out a blood curdling scream. Or was it a series of screams?

At that instant, I did not know that it was just a depraved older brother playing a silly prank.

In what must have been a matter of seconds, I turned around and flew down the stairs without bothering to touch terra firma.

Joseph – seeing that his prank had turned out a bit more full-on that he would have liked – dashed off in pursuit of me down the stairs. Of course, he was hoping to explain that this was all a joke.

George – poor kid – unaware of the specifics – but certain that I was fleeing from death itself – was frozen solid on the steps. I'm not sure if he exercised his vocal chords like I did in flight, but I reckon he hoped that no movement was the best course of action.

I rushed into our home still screaming in fright, with Joseph – beyond rattled – right behind me. Mum and Dad – once they were sure we were not under attack – were visibly upset with what happened, but chose to spare Joseph any harsh sanctions. I guess they were all a bit taken aback with the hellish din I was making.

The next day, the neighbours politely enquired if all was well. It wasn't often that the still of the night on our street was broken by the shrieking and howling of a kid under attack. But... they reasoned... who is to know what level of dysfunction resides in every decent home?

14

Bruno in the rain

Let me tell you about the day I realised just how marvellous the afterlife was going to be.

We had had some unusually heavy rains for a couple of days and I was worried about the roof leaks that I had not bothered to attend to for years. For some time, I had seen the warning signs – water marks on the ceiling, peeling paint on the walls, stubborn swaths of mould and mildew in some parts, and a buckled ceiling in my living room. But at 82, I really had a buckling spine and a miscellaneous assortment of other ailments that had me preoccupied. Repairs on the house would have to wait.

My daughter had called the previous night to check how the roof was holding up, and I tried to reassure her that it would hold for as long as I said so. But the rain seemed relentless.

As I took my bowl of soup to the living room, I glanced up

nervously at the damp, sagging ceiling and resolved to have it looked at as soon as the rain let up.

When you live alone for as long as I have, you build your life around commonplace routine. And reading a fat novel with a bowl of hot soup was one delicious part of my end-of-day routine that I looked forward to ardently.

I finished my soup faster than usual, set it aside and put my feet up to devote myself completely to the novel in hand. You may not have much, but that little is enough.

With the steady thrum of the rain on my windows, I was drifting off into that hazy, half-asleep state of languid bliss. Seemed to be quite a frequent occurrence for me these last few years – not committing to full wakefulness or to deep sleep.

And then through that lull, I heard it loud and clear.

I heard Bruno's strong and urgent bark.

Bruno was my neighbour's yellow Labrador. For a little over a decade now, I would watch him from my living room window every morning as he romped through the open green that separated our houses. On those rare occasions when I felt strong enough to go out for a stroll around the same time, he would take his frolic down a notch, just so he could walk by my side. When I would tire, he would wait patiently till I could catch my breath on the park bench. And as I headed back home, he would accompany me to my porch and then bound off again to play on the green. Sometimes I wondered if I knew any other soul as pure, noble, and devoted as that dog.

I looked at the clock. It was close to eight and the rain

had not eased. What was Bruno doing outside in this dreadful downpour?

I hobbled to the front door, opened my umbrella, braced myself and walked out onto my porch.

At that time of the night, the green was almost completely in darkness. And in the rain, it was difficult to see much. But right under the street light closest to my porch was Bruno in the rain.

He was looking at me, barking ceaselessly and making as if to run further away onto the green. I called out to him, hoping that he'd come over, so I wouldn't have to step out into the rain. But he paced in agitation around the same spot under the light, refusing to come to me.

Cursing under my breath, I took a few steps onto my porch, holding the umbrella as low as I could to protect my ears from the cold spray.

My eyes were still on Bruno when I heard behind me an almighty groan and crash. I turned around just in time to see the warped ceiling of my living room collapse under the weight of the water. The old sofa, on which I had till a few seconds ago been semi-snoozing, was buried under beams, rafters, and plasterboard. Stupefied by the near miss, I stared blankly at the gaping mess that was once my living room.

The noise had evidently been loud enough to alarm the neighbourhood. I saw a few lights come on around the green and a few concerned figures hurrying to my aid.

Before they reached me, I looked back to the light on the green, but could not see Bruno.

An hour later, I found myself still outside my house, but sitting in a van from the emergency services. Despite the deluge, they had come promptly to assess the damage, but had decided it was too unsafe to let me back into the house. So, one of them had called my daughter and I was now on the phone with her, breathlessly narrating to her my narrow escape. This was all a bit much for me and she could tell I was shaken because I wasn't letting her get a word in. I finally rounded off my story by telling her that she had Bruno to thank for still having me alive that night. And then she said, "But Daddy, Bruno died a month ago. You remember, I took you over to say one final farewell before he passed?"

I know I do not have much time left. But when it's time, there will be so many to meet on that wide open green. There will be family and friends I've missed for too long.

And... there will also be Bruno in the rain.

15

I did think of that first!

Mid-way through the movie
Bloody Hell!
Excuse me?
Bloody Hell!
You okay Bill?
I'm okay, but that's not fair!
Shhhshhhhh... Do you mind Bill? We are midway through the movie, and I don't think people are going to take kindly to you mouthing off in the middle of important dialogue.

Sorry... but how could they do this, Sam?

How could who do what Bill? Can you make yourself a bit clearer? This random commentary is throwing me off.

I'll tell you when we get out of the cinema.

Okay.

After the movie

So, what was that all about Bill?

I'm ruined Sam.

Can you speak English please?

The movie... that's my story. That was the plot of my book.

You've written a book Bill?

No Sam... but I planned to. And that bloody movie was blow-by-blow the exact plot that I had thought up years ago! Not fair!!

16

No regrets

You know son, here's some free advice. From someone who's at the end of the road. Ready for the palliative care suite. At that point of no return.

And I remind you that like the finest things in life – rain, fresh air, and sunsets – this advice, it's free!

So here goes...

I've often heard people say – "I have no regrets." Well, let me give you some news, son. That is the biggest load of bollocks you will ever hear. Nothing comes close to that. Not the biggest lie that the government dishes out to you. Not the worst corporate fraud you've heard of. Not the silliest ever self-help cliché you know.

No other falsehood... no other untruth is as untrue as that claim – "I have no regrets."

"Why, Les, why would you think so?" you ask me. No fears, mate. I'm going to tell you why.

Everybody regrets something.

Maybe he should have gone ahead with that degree in psychology when he had the time and the energy. Maybe she should have been brave and bought those shares when the market crashed. Maybe they should have taken that loan and gone on that family holiday before the accident changed it for all.

Perhaps that fella should have talked to that girl instead of slinking away in mock indifference. Perhaps she could have bit her tongue instead of mouthing off and losing her best friend for life. Perhaps they should have adopted a child before it was too late.

Maybe I should have pushed hard and mastered the violin when my fingers could do my bidding. Perhaps I should have read more novels in school. Been more disciplined with my diet. Stayed the course with the yoga. Said "sorry" more readily.

You see son, you are either a saint with no attachments or you are invested in this life. When – like the rest of us – you feel that rush of anger and that ache of loss, you will also feel that pang of regret. We are hardwired to feel our way to happiness... and to sorrow. So why not to regret?

So, the next time you hear someone declare – "I have no regrets", go ahead and smack them on the head with the nearest chair, car, or bus. That's one thing you won't have to regret!

17

Emergency c-section

It was a little after lunch when I got the call.

Dr Merrick did not waste words: "How would you like for your wife to have the baby today?"

"Today!!"

"Yes, she came in for the check-up and we found the baby in distress."

"Is she okay Doc? And the baby?"

"She's fine and the baby is fine. We just feel it's better to get the baby out without delay. How soon can you make it to the hospital?"

"It should take me an hour by train."

"Can't you get here faster?"

"Okay, let me just get in a cab and I'll try to make it in 30 minutes."

I raced out of the office, hopped into a cab, and told the

driver I needed to get to St. Andrews Hospital in 30 minutes. He did not disappoint.

Running into the maternity ward, I could see them waiting to get started with the caesarean section; a gown at the ready for me to don before entering the OR.

All prep had been done. A minute later and they would have had to start without me.

They positioned me to Agnes' right and warned me not to stray from where I stood. She seemed completely bewildered, excited, and frightened at the same time. What was supposed to be a routine check-up ended up with both of us in the OR. I held her hand and heard Dr Merrick drone on in his affable manner as he and the team got to work.

Before we knew it, our little boy was in our hands!

An hour later, they moved us from recovery to the room that Agnes and our son would use for the rest of their hospital stay.

For her, it was a 15 cm abdominal wound – much more substantial than what I expected. And that would need time to heal.

The nurses were extremely friendly and supportive. Especially given that we were recently arrived in the country, with no immediate family at hand.

It was raining outside... much like it did on our wedding day. But that was almost a year ago and oceans apart. That was six hundred guests – family and friends – sharing our special day. That was a different world.

From her bed, Agnes watched me as I sat quietly for a while, holding our son.

Tears welled up and she said, "No one with us... not one person with us at this time."

I looked out of the window, thought of family back home, looked back down at the little squirming bundle in my hand, looked up at Agnes... and smiled.

18

Bus stop conversations with a serial killer

I just heard the most extraordinary story, Dad.

What was it, Perry? Just hold on tight to the ladder, will you, while I figure out where to nail this.

You know old Mr Gribble... he was a serial killer who did time and is just out of maximum-security prison!

You mean our new neighbour, James Gribble?

Yes!

Who told you that?

He did.

Hold onto the ladder, Perry! I don't want to come crashing down... When did he tell you this?

This morning. He was sitting at the bus stop waiting for the 902 to the plaza.

When you were on your way to school?

Yes.

And what did he say?

Oh, I missed my 7:30 to school... so I sat down to wait. And he was sitting there already.

"Hi Mr Gribble" I say.

And he says, "Morning Perry, what a nice day to die!"

And I say, "Beg your pardon, Mr Gribble."

And he says, "I said, it's a nice day to die. I just know which days are right."

"How do you know, Mr Gribble?"

"Years of practice, son."

"Practising what Mr Gribble?"

"Oh, you know..." And he winked at me like I was supposed to be in on his secret.

So, I said again, "Practising what?"

And he said, "You know, helping people cross over to the other side."

I still did not get it. So, he leaned over and muttered, "I've murdered quite a few in my time, Perry... quite a few."

"What!! Mr Gribble, you killed someone?"

"Not one, Perry... no, no... I couldn't stop with just one. You know I made it a matter of principle to knock off at least one person in every port I visited."

"You were a sailor!"

"Of course, didn't you know that? All my life... hardly spent more than a couple of months at a time at home since I turned 18. Made it easy to stay one step ahead of the cops for a long time. But they got me in the end... in Singapore. I've done my 30-year stretch at maximum-security and they only let me out because I don't really have much time left. It's the cancer of the stomach."

"Come on, Mr Gribble, you are joking."

"I wouldn't joke about something like that, now, would I?"

"About the killings, how can I know you're telling me the truth?"

"I've got proof son. You want to see it?"

"I don't believe you Mr Gribble... you seem such a nice man... but show me."

"Okay well then, you know us serial killer types, we look on each kill as a trophy. We like to document such things. Keep a record."

"Yes Mr Gribble, I know... I've seen it on TV... the killer makes notches on his gun."

"Or he might keep body parts in formaldehyde."

"Yes, yes... I've seen that too in a show."

"I didn't do either. Instead, I tattooed each kill on my arm. Here, take a look."

And he rolled up his sleeve and showed me his left forearm. You won't believe it Dad... it was covered in names... each tattooed in a different style... some in red... some in blue... some in black... some with a small face hovering above the name... some with a knife or gun or rope - "the manner of death", he explained.

And you believed him?

You should have seen it, Dad!

Son, Mr Gribble has been a tattooist all his life. He's worked at the tattoo parlour in our plaza for 40 years. He moved to our street a few months ago after he retired. Has never stepped beyond this town even for a holiday all his adult life. Now pass me the hammer.

19

The interrogation

I told her to stop.

Stop what?

She didn't listen.

Mr Adams you shot the lady at point blank range. You shot her as you exited the cinema hall. Take your time, but can you tell me what happened?

I paid good money for that premiere.

So, it was a first day, first show?

Yes officer.

Which movie?

'Another Time Another Place'. Denzel Washington as a war vet.

So, you're a fan?

Yes.

Okay, you were watching this movie... and then?

This lady, she came in ten minutes into the movie and sat to my left.

And?

Why don't they just lock the doors after the movie starts? If you're not serious about watching, don't bother coming!

Okay, so what happened then?

She hauled out one large bag of chips and one large bucket of popcorn... and promptly started chomping loudly.

Wait... I thought they did away with those noisy plastic bags for chips.

Apparently... but looks like she smuggled in her own.

And then?

I asked her to be quiet.

Go on.

She didn't listen.

And?

She kept up this loud crunching and insane rustling of that blasted plastic bag. That ought to be outlawed – bag and bag holder.

And?

I tried closing my ears to cut out her din... but that was no use, officer... I was missing out on all that intense dialogue!

So?

I just had to grit my teeth through the rest of the movie.

And?

I shot her as I left.

You killed this lady because she happened to make loud eating noises during a movie?

Don't you get it?

Don't get what? Was she a seat kicker?

No.

Was she a heavy breather?

No.

Maybe she was snoring loudly as you watched?

No!!

Was she a compulsive texter?

No.

Did she have a bawling three-year-old with her?

No officer.

Did she have the need to verbalise what was happening on screen... you know, an obnoxious narrator with wisecracks for every scene?

No, no.

Did she have a weak bladder... squeezing past you every ten minutes to head for the toilet?

No.

So, after the premier of 'Another Time Another Place' – starring Denzel Washington – you pointed a gun at this lady and pulled the trigger because she ate noisily?

Officer, I can watch it again... sure... but it will never be that first viewing. That's ruined alright.

20

Showdown at Confetti Laneway

It's 1:30 am and I'm less than ten minutes from home.

A long day. So long, it's now the next day.

I'm past the wide main roads and into the dark side streets that should take me to our apartment.

It's a hot, humid night. But on my moped, it feels better. The warm air has no hold as I zip steadily closer home.

I wind past Ritchie's Corner and reach Confetti Laneway - the scene of so many of my previous skirmishes with the local pack of street dogs.

I never have a problem with them in the day. Don't know what it is. But something about the sun and the light makes me appear less threatening to this pack in the day.

But traversing their territory at 1:30 am is asking for trouble.

No one stirs in the houses on either side of the lane-way, which is only partially lit by streetlights spread unevenly along its length. It's just the dogs lying in various positions of repose deep in the shadows thrown by old trees.

One of the dogs stirs as the soft purr of my moped becomes louder and as my dim headlight becomes visible. Another cocks his head and sits up. A third literally leaps out of his slumber as if caught off guard.

I'm about thirty yards from the pack.

A couple of them let out deep and unsettling growls. There is no mistaking their intentions. I must pay for the audacity of this foray across the line of control.

Two dogs start jogging into the centre of the street. They will get me even if the others don't. A third darts out of the shadows and begins a direct sprint towards me. A fourth rabid hound scurries along the side of the laneway looking to launch a flank attack.

They are now barking with a ferocity that would dissuade even the most insane adventurer from pursuing this futile charge.

But it's been a long day... a long night... so I rev up the little moped and swerve past the first mutt that snaps furiously at my heel.

Crazed by the miss, he gives chase from behind even as his unhinged buddy launches himself virtually off the ground to target my upper calf. Instinctively, I kick hard, and my foot meets his stubborn, unyielding head. Almost losing my balance with the force of the recoil, I take my eyes off the last two dogs in the centre of the street.

I recover quickly and brace myself for the final hurdle.

Street dogs are a resilient bunch. They live and die by their daring. And these were not about to let this impudent thief go by.

Knowing in that split second that there was no way I could ride around them, I throttle hard and push right into them with my legs spreadeagled as high as I could without losing balance again.

Jaws snap fast and hard millimetres from flesh and bone. In a moment, I'm past the deranged devils and speeding for my life.

They give chase for a few seconds but pull away as I reach the end of the laneway.

I live to fight another day.

"Long day?" Mum asks as I walk into our apartment. She and Dad had stayed up.

"Oh, it was alright" I say as I scan the kitchen to see what I can sample from the dinner I missed.

21

Before the tour

That was the year Christine got married.

Your daughter?

Yes.

Okay Lyn. And what year was that?

Oh... you got me there! You will have to check with Don. These days I'm fairly useless with dates, months and years.

Not a problem Lyn. He's stepped out to speak to my colleague... so I'll check with him when he's back.

I was hoping Christine could have joined us today to have a look at the room. I so rely on her for her advice.

No issues Lyn. I can organise another tour of the facility for Christine before you make your decision.

That would be nice.

Does she live close to your place?

Only 15 minutes away.

That's handy.

Yes, three days a week she drops off George on her way to work and picks him up in the afternoon. George just turned two. He is the highlight of our week! I don't know what Don and I would do if we did not have to look after him those three days.

Christine must be so thankful that she has the two of you to help out like this.

Oh... it's nothing. Christine is all we have. We'd do anything for her. And she is doing such a fine job with George. You know her marriage did not last. We knew it right from the start... but whatever his faults, he's still George's father... so it must be tough on the little fellow... and on Christine.

They have you and Don to lean on. So that's a blessing.

Yes... they do.

Give me a moment Lyn. I'll just step out to see if Don is finished.

Oh, there you are Don. I've been chatting with your wife in my office. Just wanted to see if you had finished up here.

Oh hi... yes. Are we heading to see the room now?

Yes, in a moment. Did you have any questions so far?

Heaps... but I'll get to that later. I'm still reeling from that discussion of the finances that your colleague was kind enough to have with me. I had no idea that aged care could be this complicated!

Yeah... tell me about it! But don't worry. Your financial adviser should be able to make things clearer once you are ready.

Yes, I'm going to need some of that translated into simple English!

And your wife mentioned that she was keen for your daughter, Christine to also have a look at the room. Happy to organise that as well.

She said that, did she?

Yes... and before I forget, please also email me a copy of Lyn's assessment report.

Sure... will do. By the way, your colleague gave me a quick rundown of the staffing ratios, daily routine, access to doctors, kitchen, and dining facilities... but I missed checking with her what the visiting hours would be for family members and what were the recreational or social activities that you organise for the residents.

Sure. Visiting hours are from 1 to 3 pm, seven days a week. And I will email you the full list of recreational activities we have onsite... there's so much that Lyn will be able to get involved with here.

Thank you. It's just that she really looks forward to talking to people. Ever since she broke her hip eight years ago, she's been restricted somewhat.

Yes Don... that can be a challenge for those with limited mobility. But apart from regular outdoor excursions, we've got chess, cards, Scrabble, the choir, art class, the Tai Chi group, volunteer groups, there's a very active Book club here... even some gardening... so there is always something to mark off on the calendar.

That's good to know. It's difficult even contemplating having to put her in here... away from me. But I'm running out of options.

Yes Don... we fully understand how difficult this can be for the families. But let's go get Lyn and look at the room. It's not the same one that she will get when she is admitted, but it's the same configuration as what she will get.

Okay, let's do that. And by the way, don't bother about organising any other tour for us later. This will be it.

Oh, I thought Lyn was keen for your daughter to...

Christine and my grandson died ten years ago in a car crash.

Don... I'm so sorry. It's just that Lyn said...

I know... don't worry about it. Will the room overlook the gardens?

22

Outside office hours

I noticed something was wrong when he called one morning to let me know that he would be an hour late.

Hemant was one of our experienced hands at our little call centre. Just hitting thirty, he was a nice bloke. Single, stable, and committed to the job. Well-liked by the younger ones. Respected by all. And Hemant was never late. But I guess, there's always a first time for everything.

I made as if I was quite annoyed, and he mumbled profuse apologies. He walked into the office at ten o'clock, looking a bit jaded and worn out. Very unlike Hemant.

I let it pass.

A few days later, he was late again. This time he walked in stiff, sore, and limping as if he'd been through a marathon the previous day.

I walked up to his desk, let him finish his call and started:

Hemant, what's up? You look like you've just done the marathon!

Oh, hi Maya... I'm sorry I'm late. Had to help a friend with moving house last evening. Did my back in trying to heave one of those large sofas.

Okay Hemant.... but as Team Leader I cannot be excusing you every time. You've been here for years. I just won't be able to keep the younger ones in line. If you are unwell, you can call in sick.

Understood Maya... won't happen again.

A week later, he called in sick.

I saw him again after two days. He had a black eye and a bandaged left hand.

Sparring match gone wrong, he said.

That afternoon, he had to leave after coughing up blood.

Next morning, I did not let him settle at his desk, but took him straight into my room.

What is going on with you Hemant? You are getting me worried?

Nothing Maya... I told you... was sparring with my friend ... should have been more careful.

Okay... but you haven't been yourself lately. Is everything alright with you?

Never better Maya! (His eyes had a silly but feverish gleam.)

You know you can tell me Hemant. After all these years,

I would have thought you'd know that I'm not just Team Leader... you can tell me if something is going wrong.

Maya, really... never felt better!

Knock it off Hemant...I'm not a newbie you can brush off. You rock up late... something you've never done in all this time you've been with us. You limp and stumble ... you sport a black eye... a wound on your hand... you cough up blood... What next?

Okay Maya... you really want to know?

Of course, I do.

You're not going to believe me, though.

Try me.

Okay... here goes: You read the story in the press... a month ago maybe... about two would-be robbers tied up and left outside the jewellery shop they had planned to rob opposite Emerald flyover? And no one knew how and who.

Yes... and?

You remember the story a few weeks ago of a wife-beater getting thrashed by a stranger at Central Station right in front of his wife, who he had just struck.

No... but what's all this got to do with you?

Okay... you heard of the brawl outside the Modern Art Museum two nights ago? These guys had pounced onto this one homeless guy like a pack of wild animals, and he only escaped with his life because an unknown passer-by belted the boys out of there?

That I heard about... but you're losing me.

That was all me, Maya.

Sorry... you mean you beat up those bullies?

Yes.

And the wife-beater?

Yes.

And you rounded up those robbers?

Would-be robbers... yes.

Okay... you were right... I don't believe you.

But somebody must step up, Maya! We can't just watch things happen to us.

Are you freaking nuts, Hemant? You are a bloody call centre operator. You talk to mums and dads about insurance policies, electricity bills, home internet plans, mobile plans, and streaming services. You are not bloody Batman!!

No... I don't wear a cape.

Okay, so all is not lost! But seriously, Hemant, this messiah complex will get you killed! I'm guessing you've been prowling the streets looking for trouble for a month now? And look at the shape you are in!!

I boxed in school and at university, Maya. I can take care of myself.

You need your head examined Hemant; I mean it. Okay, why are you doing that?

Doing what?

Why are you nodding like that Hemant, are you hearing things I cannot? Is that some kind of self-talk?

Not everyone gets it, I accept.

Stop Hemant! Whatever this is. Delusion, paranoia, psychosis? I don't know. Whatever it is... you've got to stop.

I'm just getting started Maya!

I cannot believe we are having this conversation!! Hemant, you really are a piece of work!

And then the phone rang.

That conversation with Hemant was to be our last as colleagues. I was made redundant with that phone call and, in the sheer embarrassment of having to clear off before the new shift, I missed saying farewell to Hemant and his crew.

I fought a few of my own battles for some months after and only thought of Hemant again when I read the local news story one morning about a call centre operator by the name of Hemant Kumar who was found dead by a truck depot on Alpine Road with his head smashed in. I couldn't believe what I had read. Was it my vigilante friend? I had his number on speed dial, so it did not take me long to find out.

Hello, Hemant here.

Oh my God... that's you, Hemant! Maya here. I just read about a 'Hemant' killed last night.

Hi Maya... how good to hear from you! Yes, this is the tenth call I've got this morning... all asking me if I'm dead. No... it's some other poor bastard. 'Hemant Kumar' is not exactly an obscure name.

Ha... you're right Hemant! I was just so mortified to read the story. Just thinking about our last conversation before I got fired!

Yes, Maya... I remember.

So, are you still the deranged do-gooder?

No Maya.

What!! No more the call centre crime fighter?

No Maya.

What changed?

You won't believe me Maya.

I've got a feeling I will.

A week after we spoke, I met this girl and...

Okay, I believe you!

23

Pulled over

It was a quiet December morning that was about to turn bad.

I was driving home after a brief stop at the shops with my three-year-old daughter, Elena.

Empty roads... clear, blue skies... the start of a week away from work... what was there not to like about that morning!

And then I saw the lights and heard the siren.

A glance at my speedometer told me that I was in trouble... over ten kilometres per hour above the speed limit.

I pulled over to the side of the road.

The cop pulled up behind me and stepped out.

I was already in dangerous territory – with nine demerit points on my driver's license for previous infringements (they are not pertinent to this story).

My mind was racing... it was holiday period; so apart from a hefty fine for speeding, I would also be looking at a possible six more demerit points. That would mean automatic suspension of my license for three months!!

The skies took on a hue of black grey... or so I thought.

Elena – oblivious to the sudden change in my fortunes – smiled back at me as I looked over my shoulder.

The cop looked like in his mid-fifties.

I rolled down my window and waited.

"Morning, sir", he started – clipped and no-nonsense – "Any reason why you were going at 75 in a 60 zone?"

"Morning, Officer. Was it 75!! Didn't seem like that at all."

"Can I see your license please?"

"Sure, Officer, here you go."

"Okay... that's all good, but I'm going to have to write you a ticket."

"I'm sorry Officer... really... won't happen again."

"That's not going to cut it, sir. And its double demerits."

"It's Christmas time, Officer. Please, a little leniency?"

He was about to knock back my plea when he spotted her in the back seat.

"Oh! Hullo there, young lady!"

Sitting upright in her booster seat, Elena looked at him with a direct, open gaze.

She was sure her dad was in trouble, but not so sure that this awfully nice man in blue was going to be the cause of said trouble.

She smiled.

"You're a happy camper back there."

I looked back at Elena. She gave the cop one of her

disarming doe-eyed looks, all framed by chubby cheeks and a large mop of curly hair.

He hesitated for a second.

And then... the book he had pulled out went right back into his pocket!

"I wouldn't want to mess up her Christmas now, would I?"

I looked at him, not sure how best to respond.

"I'll let this one go. But you had better not be caught speeding any time soon."

"Thank you, Officer... not going to happen again."

He looked back at Elena and beamed.

"Honey, you tell your dad to take it slow."

And that's it... he was gone.

I quickly started up and moved on (just in case he decided to change his mind).

As I neared home, I looked into the rear view and Elena was still silently trying to figure out what that was all about. She caught my eye and smiled.

It was a quiet December morning... and it turned out good.

24

Miracle at St. Michael's

Father Paul raised the host and said the Eucharistic prayer: "Through him, with him, in him, in the unity of the Holy Spirit, all glory and honour is yours, almighty Father, forever and ever."

The congregation responded with a half-hearted "Amen."

I glanced up at the massive bronze crucifix that hung from the church ceiling, just above the altar. I had always wondered why anybody would choose to hang such a heavy piece right above the altar!

The low creak turned louder. It seemed to come from up there... above the altar. It was the metal rod that held the crucifix to the ceiling. It was giving way! It must have held that crucifix in place for ages... many more than my 11 years on the planet.

I looked up quickly to Mum and Dad on my right. No alarm on their faces. Did they not see and hear what I did?

I looked back up at the crucifix. Yes, it definitely seemed to shake and shudder as its anchoring to the ceiling started coming loose.

Father Paul standing right below did not notice either. What was wrong with all of them! That crucifix was certainly going to come down crashing on him and the altar.

Judging by what it must have weighed, this was going to be the last mass that our beloved parish priest was going to be celebrating... ever!

Somebody had to do something. I looked around. Not one responsible adult seemed to have woken up.

"For the kingdom, the power and the glory are yours now and for ever," they all recited matter-of-factly.

Were they all under some spell? Perhaps, no one would know till that crucifix plummeted and killed our poor priest.

If no one but me could see what was going on, then maybe it was just up to me to do something.

But what could a little 11-year-old do?

The metal rod could not hold out much longer. The crack that ran through it widened... the crucifix swayed unsteadily... any second now and it would come loose!

I stood up and launched myself up into the air. This wasn't some frantic, futile leap. It was full flight. I could feel my body clear the ground.

I was soaring fast. But the oncoming threat had slowed every frame down.

I was now twenty feet in the air and zooming straight to the crucifix.

With a loud sharp crack, the rod snapped completely, and the crucifix dropped.

I heard the collective gasp from the congregation below me (at last, they could see what was really happening here!). Father Paul, who had his head bowed down, now swivelled up to look with pure terror in his eyes at the colossal crucifix about to end his days. It fell fast.

But just about five feet from his cowering form, it stopped in mid-air. I had reached it in time... and had heaved it up with my bare hands... up and away from the altar and certain disaster.

"Henry!" I could hear Mum's voice, as if from a distance.

The TV news story for tomorrow was going to be unprecedented. "Miracle at St. Michael's! Local boy defies gravity to save local parish priest from certain death!" "In what must rank as a world-first, 300 parishioners at a Sunday morning catholic service witnessed the yet-to-be-explained feat of a young boy flying unaided to hold off a falling crucifix that had come loose from the ceiling."

"Henry!" It was Mum's urgent, insistent voice.

"Henry!" Mum hissed as quietly and as clearly as she could. I turned to my right as she tugged at my sleeve.

"What Mum?"

"Peace be with you."

As we drove out of church after mass, Mum looked at me and asked, "Daydreaming again at mass, Henry?"

25

Gut feel

I don't like him.

What!

I don't trust him.

Why?

I'm not signing the contract with him.

Missy, you can't arrive at such a conclusion after having talked to the guy for hardly five minutes!

That's enough for me. I saw him in his home.

And so?

Did you see the paintings he had hung up in his living?

Yes... I thought they looked nice.

They were not hung level. Not one of them! A guy who does not adjust his own picture frames on his own wall... who can stand the sight of them infuriatingly askew every day that he walks past them... that is someone I would not want to be signing a contract with.

26

After the funeral

Mum, you're still up?

Yes, Liv. I couldn't sleep.

It's been a long day, Mum.

Uhmm... For the life of me, I cannot remember where your father saved it.

You're looking for something on his laptop?

Yes, Liv.

Can't it wait till the morning? You must be tired.

No... not really. You and your brother did such a fine job with all the arrangements. I just did not have a thing to worry my head over.

Actually Mum, Belinda from the funeral directors – she is the one that Gabe and I have to thank. She really made it all so seamless.

Yes. I loved the simple floral arrangement they used in the church.

Yes Mum... and the no-fuss timber coffin... Dad would have approved.

I know Liv... these last few years, he was always going on about not spending too much on his funeral.

We didn't Mum. Even with the hearse, the audio-visual that Belinda put together, the buffet, the plot at Larwood... all of it still came well below what Gabe and I estimated.

I just loved that Gabe managed to get their Chrysler for the hearse... your dad would have enjoyed that last ride.

Yes Mum.

And Father Chris – his homily was just so right.

Yes Mum. He's a good priest.

But Liv... I just can't seem to find this file.

Here, let me try. Do you know which folder?

No... your dad told me ... but I have clean forgotten.

Okay, what is the file name?

Something starting with 'L'.

What is it ... a Word document? A PowerPoint? A photograph?

No... it's an audio file... an MP3.

Okay... let me see. It's not here in the C drive. It's not on the desktop. What was the MP3 about?

It was what he wanted us to play during the funeral mass. For the post-communion. He was very specific. It was Beethoven's slow movement from his last string quartet.

What! I did not know about this Mum! You should have told me earlier... I would have located it... or Gabe would have.

I know Liv. It just slipped my mind completely. It's certainly music I would have heard your dad play at home many times before. But you know me. To your father's undimmed horror, after all those years married to the man, I'm still not sure what the difference between an allegro and an adagio is. He called it the cardinal sin that could never be forgiven – my not understanding the basics of classical music.

Okay let me search with B.

I should have told you.

There it is! '*Beethoven_Lento assai cantante e tranquillo*'. See... he prefixed the name of the piece with 'Beethoven'.

Oh... thank you Liv! I wish I had thought to check this before.

Let me Google this. Okay... it's from the String Quartet No. 16 in F major... the last major work he composed... almost his farewell to the world... this movement, it's about seven to eight minutes long... apparently one of the most beautiful slow movements that Beethoven composed.

What a shame, Liv. I wish I had remembered! You know how essential his music was to your father.

Don't worry, Mum. You obviously were dealing with a lot. Fixing the funeral music was not right up there on the list. But why don't we listen to it now? I'm sure Dad is listening in too.

Okay, let's do that.

Ahh... I remember this!

Wow! This is such a serene piece of music, Mum! Really heartfelt... transcendent!

Remind me again, Liv, what did we actually play at the post-communion instead of this?

I think it was *'Abide with me.'*

Oh Lord, Liv... Looks like I'm in for a stern talking-to when I get to meet your dad next!

27

Haggling with a pro

Dad, can I get an Instagram account?

No, Elena.

Why not?

We discussed this before.

That was when I was thirteen. I'm fourteen now.

And it's still a 'No'.

Why?

You don't need one.

I can think of lots of things that we don't need, but that we still get!

It's not safe.

All the girls in our group are on Instagram.

The 'common cold' is common. That does not make it good for you.

Really Dad... that's so "boomer"!

It's a free-for-all. No filters... nothing.

But I will be sensible. You know I will.

Of course, you will, but it's not safe. There are weirdos out there... bullying, stalking, and harassing others.

I can keep my account private.

But your profile is public.

C'mon Dad, I'm not a kid anymore! I'm so out-of-the-loop without it.

Whatever happened to email or text messaging?

We use those... but I'm missing out on what my group is sharing on Instagram.

That's okay Elena... you don't have to be in every group.

You don't understand!

It's still a 'No' Elena.

Till when?

Till you are ready.

Next year?

We'll see.

Okay, at least let me get on WhatsApp. No random users there.

Okay... but no Instagram.

Thanks Dad.

Wait...what just happened there?

28

Roadside memorial

My son, Gareth, he did not want to ride his bike back home in the dark.

His friend's father offered to drop him back to our place.

They found both bodies ten metres from the crash. The impact was such.

It's been eight years now... he would have turned twenty this June.

But each June, we still tie a bunch of flowers to the post nearest the site of the crash. It's the 'Start Freeway' sign just after you cross St. Mary's.

In the first few years, I brought magnolias simply because I liked them. But they wilted fast. So, I've been partial to sunflowers since. They are so much sturdier than the magnolias.

One June, we turned up and found that the city council had moved the post over a hundred metres further down the road. No particular reason why! We just had to improvise that year and stick in a sturdy branch from a tree. But the next year, they had the post back where it was meant to be.

29

A classical musician with misplaced loyalties

So, maestro, when you are not making classical music on the podium – along with your absolutely fabulous orchestra, what music do you listen to?

Oh... pretty much all the usual suspects in pop, country, soul, folk... and some rock.

And your all-time favourite band would be?

Mmmmm... I would have to say ABBA.

Sorry... maestro?

ABBA.

You mean the Dancing Queen ABBA??!!!!

Yes.

The Mamma Mia ABBA??!!!!

Yes... yes... there's only one ABBA... but you seem surprised?

No maestro... it's just that I may have been expecting The Beatles or one of the other more serious bands... But ABBA??!!

Why not ABBA?

No offence maestro, but if there are more cheesy lyrics in pop music than ABBA, I haven't heard them.

Ahhha... not every great pop supergroup needs to tick off the box of being great lyricists as well.

I agree maestro... but you really can't be serious... not many can take ABBA seriously!!

Sure... they did not seed a revolution in their audiences with their lyrics. But the music is not always about the lyrics, is it?

Yes maestro... but...

Listen to their melodies... their wall of sound approach to instrumentation and recording... their obsession with every little detail in the recording studio.

Yes maestro... but not many would see them as anything more than gaudy entertainers.

And what did you think most classical music composers saw their role as? Pretty much the same thing... entertainers who perfected the craft of hooking audiences with some mysterious, magical concoction of melody, rhythm, and drama. And I'm not fussed about their gaudy outfits. Have you seen what David Bowie wore... or Liberace... or Prince... or Elton John?

That's true maestro... but there's a reason why the greats are respected for the sophistication of their lyrics. There's a reason why a Bob Dylan is worshipped... or a Bruce Springsteen or a Leonard Cohen.

And there's also a reason why simplicity is the highest form of art.

You must be referring to the one-dimensional nature of many ABBA songs.

Wow!! So much condescension for one of the most successful pop groups of all time! They had to have got some things right.

You mistake me maestro... how do I put it... I'm just a bit perplexed that an artist of your calibre would find ABBA so... compelling.

Believe me, there is something symphonic and operatic about ABBA. That's the way they leveraged multi-track recordings to create such thrilling aural textures... such life-affirming rhythms... such high-octane crescendos. You say 'one-dimensional'... and I say that's furthest from the truth. In the emotional content of their songs too, there is always a melancholic, bittersweet undercurrent... even to their most upbeat hits.

Maestro... forgive me... but this is perhaps the most uncool view I've heard in a long time!!

I get it... it is uncool to be an ABBA fan in some circles. Apparently, it only means anything if the lyrics split atoms.

I didn't say that maestro... but you are really making it hard for yourself if you go on about ABBA.

So, let me get this straight, just because Shakespeare is the pinnacle of the English language, am I to feel bad if I also enjoy a good old detective novel that happens to be a bestseller?

But detective novels fade with the season. Today's bestseller is forgotten tomorrow. Shakespeare is for all time.

Of course, Shakespeare is for all time. But there's longevity in ABBA as well. They stopped recording as a group in 1982. My grandkids have them on their playlists now.

I don't know maestro... it's going to be difficult for me to yield ground to ABBA.

Well, there you have it... I've been a fan of ABBA for decades... and I'm too old to bother about who agrees with me now.

Of course, Maestro... pardon me if I went off on a tangent there. So, let's move on... the grapevine has it that you and the orchestra have something special planned for your season opening concert this year?

Yes... we open with Copland's *Appalachian Spring* and end with Beethoven's *Pastoral Symphony*. Both works celebrating the spiritual strength that comes from being close to nature. In between, we premiere a new work – and that's a surprise worth waiting for. But who knows, this interview has got me thinking... I might just throw in an orchestral medley of ABBA's greatest hits as a warm-up. Now that would wake them up, alright... Wouldn't it!

30

Embers

The last time I met Oscar was also the first time I'd seen him in over a decade.

I was about to start a leisurely Saturday lunch alone at my favourite neighbourhood restaurant, when the guest at the table behind me called out to the waiter. I recognised the voice immediately. It was my one time buddy from my days in charity fundraising, Oscar Romero.

Born in 1980 in El Salvador, he was named after the famous social revolutionary, the Archbishop of San Salvador who was assassinated while celebrating mass that same year.

By his early teens, Oscar had begun to lose interest in schooling even as he became more actively involved in projects for social justice and poverty alleviation in his community. By the time I got to know him, he was already a social work veteran.

In the two years that I hustled unsuspecting commuters

and passers-by with fervent pleas for charitable donations, Oscar and I became close friends. In the cut and thrust of fundraising, you really needed to lean on someone just to keep your spirits up. That is because charity fundraising was and is a blood sport.

Oscar and I were face-to-face fundraisers recruited by one of the fastest growing marketing agencies contracted for charity fundraising in Sydney. We focused on soliciting one-off donations and ongoing commitments from members of the public. And we did this on the street, in shopping malls, at train stations, bus stops, and parks. A few of the lucky ones on our team escaped the midday heat and made unsolicited phone calls to potential donors from the air-conditioned comfort of the call centre. If someone hung up on them, they could swear and scream freely. If someone ignored us on the street, we still had to grin and carry on.

We raised funds for every imaginable cause - cancer research, homeless shelters, saving the planet, emergency relief, animal protection, mental health, religious institutions, children's charities, the arts.

As with any type of sales process, we had to work through the funnel, which typically looked like 30 initial interactions leading to about 15 extended conversations, resulting in one actual sign up. It was bloody hard work. And that is why the churn rate of fundraisers was so high. Not many lasted more than six months.

We were given a commission for every successful donor signed up. That was it. No salary.

The agency did spend time training us on how to get the attention of a passer-by, how to engage, how to leverage the psychology of selling to draw out a commitment, negotiate and close. But nothing can prepare young backpackers for the soul crushing string of rejections that you'd have to contend with on a daily basis as a fundraiser.

Worse still, the agency did not have much patience for non-performance. You did not bring in new donors in a week or two, and you were unceremoniously kicked out. For Oscar and I (and for most of the international students or travellers), who were employed as casual workers, this was our main income. So, the stakes were high. This often led to poor behaviour in our team – everything from manipulation of potential donors to coercion to downright aggression.

For Oscar though, this was not some desperate game of survival. It was a chance to get people to think beyond themselves. That is why the rejections did not upset him. He also had an easy charm that helped him chat up almost anybody.

Both of us lasted longer than most. But when I left to take up a 'real' job, Oscar stayed on for another six months before moving to Cambodia to help build houses for remote communities. Two months into that project, he fell off some scaffolding and spent the rest of the year recuperating from multiple fractures.

From there, he tried to make it work behind a desk, but gave up after a frustrating 18 months in some administrative role in a regulatory agency.

Almost on the rebound, he hopped through Asia and Africa for the next five years, working with an international aid agency, building makeshift shelters, supporting refugee resettlement, mobilising education efforts in remote communities, training and managing volunteers. Along the way, he met a girl who also shared his sense of outrage at all the forms of oppression that he had in his sights. They managed to stay together for a couple of years before she decided one morning to go back to her home in Oslo. He told me, as we finished our last drink at the restaurant, that he had not heard from her since.

We rose to leave, and I noticed for the first time that Oscar was out of shape and walked with a slight limp. That, he explained, was the result of a hang glider accident eight months ago – crushed bones in his shoulder and both arms, sternum broken in two places, six broken ribs. With all the metal rods, plates, and screws in him, he was sure he'd be setting off security alarms at airports for a long time to come.

As we shook hands outside the restaurant to head our separate ways, I threw in the question I'd been holding back the whole evening. I asked him if he had changed at all since our days in fundraising. He seemed stumped by the question, but paused and said, "Funny you asked me, because that was something I've been thinking of a lot lately. I think I know what's been happening to me all along. I've been everywhere that needed me and yet I've never really belonged anywhere, to anyone. I was once a churchgoer. But the church stayed the same; I changed. And mind you, not for the better. So it will be interesting to know at which point in my old age... if I get to be old... at which point I will regret having turned away from the opportunity to belong. Because I suspect I will regret it. All in all, I think I've learnt to lower my expectations. Of people. Of institutions. Of life. It's not that I've become more cynical. But the colours are more muted these days."

Oscar never got that chance to regret anything. He died a month later of septic shock after a sudden, unexplained infection. It took a few days for the medical staff to find next of kin; made more difficult because he had been out of work for a good two years.

31

Running into the past

Who was that?

My classmate from Oak Grove.

Wow! That's a long time ago. Have you met since you left?

No.

No wonder you looked so startled. And he seemed so happy to have recognised you after all these years.

Yes... Class of '94. He was what you'd call a guy who slipped under the radar... unremarkable, inconspicuous, ordinary. Not the brightest. Not the funniest. Not even the meanest. Just one of those stodgy characters with a serious, insipid face.

Now you're being mean!

No, really. Haven't you had that type in your school?

Yes, I know what you mean. But he seemed genuinely happy to have spotted you, recognised you, and reconnected with you.

Yes, I know.

And he seemed to remember all your exploits in school. Was quite chuffed to have been in your inner circle of kids all those years.

Yes, that's the problem.

What's the problem?

He remembered so much about me. I even spoke to him for a good ten minutes just then. And for the life of me, I could not... and still cannot recollect his name!

32

Bedtime story

Daddy, why does God have favourites?

No, Elena, he doesn't have favourites. He loves us all equally.

Really?

Yes, we just experience it differently.

But why do some people have all the fun and get away with it?

You mean, doing bad things?

Yes.

Don't be so sure that they get away with it. And who's to know – some might even feel sorry that they did the wrong thing.

And why do some other people do everything right and are still unhappy?

You are asking some very challenging questions, girl!

I don't think it's fair, Daddy.

Okay, how do I explain this simply?

You can't Daddy... I just know... it does not make sense.

You're right, I cannot explain it. There's a lot in life that's beyond our understanding, Elena. But let me tell you a story. That should explain it.

Okay, what's the story?

A certain man had two sons...

33

Pedestrian at fault

I was just about to make the turn into the street that led out of the slums when I saw him crossing. A little scruffy schoolboy, dashing across the road without an even sideways glance to check for oncoming traffic.

I was too close to swerve... but swerve I did. And my bike and I parted ways.

Picking myself off the dusty road, I could smell the blood on my grazed left arm and felt the sharp stab of pain in my sprained ankle.

The bike lay sprawled on the side of the road, away from the bus, truck, and cars that motored past me, unruffled by the minor mishap.

The bike could wait.

I hobbled over to the schoolboy who had crouched over into a grotesque ball on the road, as if bracing for impact. I grabbed him by the shirt and shouted into his frightened face.

"What the hell is wrong with you!! Could you not look before crossing?"

And that little rogue mumbled back immediately, "Sorry, sir. My mother just died. My mind was not on the road."

I let go of his shirt.

My anger intensified to a point almost uncontrollable.

This boy had the unblinking eyes of a crafty survivor. For him to stoop so low as to fob me off with a sob story like that was just the worst kind of crassness.

Utterly disgusted, I turned away, picked up my bike and rode off without looking back.

How could he say something like that! Couldn't he have just offered a simple apology? Did he think I was some half-baked sucker to fall for something like that!! Why did he have to be so bleeding deceitful? Wasn't it obvious to him that there was no way his story sounded plausible? No way that he was actually distracted by grief. No possible way.

Because if it was true... if it was real... then...

34

Bound hand and foot

I'd finished trimming the backyard hedge just before she got to the balcony. Wasn't really in the mood for any kind of constructive feedback: "Honey, a little bit more on the right." Or "The hedge's not level, baby."

She took one look at the hedge, and I could sense without looking in her direction that she was trying hard to refrain from making any comment.

I had moved onto weeding along the fence.

The pollen from the grass was already sending me into fits of sneezing. But this was spring. What else could you expect?

I'd been at it since seven in the morning, and in that time, she'd put through two sets of washing out to dry in the patio.

The kids were still asleep.

My knees throbbed as I bent close to the ground, determined to get those blasted weeds out at the roots. But I had a good half of the fence on this side and the full fence on the other two sides to get through.

Weeding is not rocket science. But it is never ending. Of course, you stop weeding when you die. But till then?

You pounce on these sorts of infernal tasks with the futile hope that you can keep on top of things. But that backyard is obstinate. In two weeks, I'll find myself on my knees again, tugging at fresh weeds that refuse to yield. In two weeks, I'll be walking around in irregular circles in the backyard again, doing the lawn mowing. In one week, there will be a broken fence paling to replace, a printer that refuses to print, a vacuum cleaner that plays up, a Wi-Fi connection that goes patchy, a bathroom that needs repainting, a flat pack that refuses to be put together painlessly, a garage that needs de-cluttering, a house that needs decluttering, a life that...

So where did that simple life go? When did inviting family and friends to dinner imply a week of frenzied cleaning and a full night and day of chaotic cooking? When did a family holiday become more stressful to plan and execute than all the built-up stress that it was meant to release? When did inanimate objects – cars, houses, laptops, phones, appliances, clothes, furniture – make greater claims on me than I on them?

Sitting on my haunches now, I surveyed the weed-free fence line.

I'm sure another bloke might find that therapeutic. But that's not me. Music? Yes therapeutic. A good movie? Yes. A good book? Yes. But weeding and mowing a bloody implacable backyard? Sorry mate, not in my scheme of things!

I looked back at the balcony, and she had re-emerged after

a cruelly intensive session cleaning the grouting on the floor tiles. She looked tired, but she smiled back at me.

"Honey", she said, "You've done well with the weeding. It looks even better than the last time you attacked it. Why don't you come in for a cup of coffee? And then maybe you can have another go at the hedge; looks a bit uneven from where I'm standing."

35

Rock bottom

9:30 am

Fred, who was that on the call?

TRC. It's not looking good, Hector.

What did they say?

A lot... but the short version is that they are pulling out of the deal.

Holy cow! You can't let that happen.

Apparently, there is not much that I can do. The contract allows them to pull out. They are not convinced that we are adding value.

So, you are down half a million if this falls through!

Yes, and it's not "if". They are sending through a written confirmation shortly.

Mate, you are in some serious trouble.

I know. Will have to break the news to Daniella at head office.

11.00 am

Hector, you remember that proposal for SMC?

Yes... what about it?

They went with another firm.

Gosh, Fred. This is one thing after another!

I knew it was a long shot, Hector.

But it was in your sales pipeline!

Yes, unfortunately.

Fred, not to be blunt about it, but you are in a deep hole here.

Tell me about it, Hector. This day is not getting any better!

6:00 pm

Okay Fred, it's a wrap for me.

Sure Hector. See you tomorrow.

So, Fred, how are you holding up? I heard that your application for the new position got knocked back?

Wow, everybody seems to know about it! I just got to know five minutes ago.

Sorry mate. I know it must be tough... especially with all that you've got on your plate on the home front. When it rains it pours, uh?

It's pouring alright today.

Can't recall when last you had such a bad day.

It's never all bad Hector.

7:00 pm

Fred glances at the text message from Hector: "Did you check out the stock exchange before close? It's been a bloodbath today. Credo Corp had its fastest and steepest fall in a day. Irreversible they say. I know you had put in quite a bit into that stock... sorry mate... just when you think you've hit rock bottom..."

10:30 pm

Fred reaches his apartment after spending a couple of hours in the cancer ward at the hospital, by Mrs Fred's bedside.

He's too tired... too overwhelmed to rustle up some dinner. He splashes some water on his face, dims the lights, switches on the turntable, settles back into his sofa in the corner, closes his eyes, and listens intently to the opening of Schubert's 'Unfinished' Symphony.

From the depths, the strings surface quietly, the oboe and clarinet sing the first theme, and the cellos bring in that timeless melody.

Yes, he thinks to himself, as tears stream down – even when every possibility cannot be lived out, even when the dream disintegrates, there is always something to cling to. It's never all bad.

11:30 pm

Fred dreams that he is falling without landing.

36

Out of character

You know Sean, I've been thinking about what you said just before the waiter came over. You said that your many years have taught you that people don't really change. I get that it's difficult. But I don't buy it that they never change. I get that a lot of so-called change is pure delusion. But there are some who can surprise you by doing something so uncharacteristic that it's nothing short of miraculous.

You don't seem convinced? Well, let me give you an example from my many years.

My Dad. He was your typical white-collar. Did all he could at the office. Fought some ferocious battles for his company. Cleaned up a lot of messes for his teams. But he was not the guy you'd see rolling up his sleeves to cook up a dinner at home. Or one who'd get enthusiastic about gardening. Or dabbling around the house with DIY projects.

But one monsoon, we discovered that our tree in the back-yard was infested with blanket worms. It must have been the wet weather. It may have been because it was a drumstick tree, which is prone to such infestations. I cannot recall exactly how we landed up with that problem. But the tree was too far gone to save and there was the risk of the infestation spreading.

Dad came home one evening, got out of his sharp business attire, picked up a small sturdy machete, and he just hacked away at the tree for a good hour or so. The worms dropped around him and on him. And if you know what I'm talking about, contact with those hairy little devils leads to really painful skin irritation.

By the end of the day, our blanket worm problem was ended. The backyard was once again safe for us kids. But that night I saw Dad lying on his stomach, shirtless, and Mum applying some sort of home remedy cream to his shoulders and back that were covered with angry, burning, raised welts.

That's the only clear memory I have of him doing any sort of major backyard clean-up. But there you have it.

Another time, our sofa set needed more than just a steam clean. The upholstery had faded beyond redemption. But the frame was solid.

Dad bought new fabric, took apart the old upholstery and single-handedly reupholstered the whole sofa set without a manual to go by... and this is long before you could look it up on YouTube tutorials. We were too young to be of much use to the project at the time. But I know we used that sofa set for many more years after.

Out of work for months one time, Dad went back to the company he had just resigned from; just so he could put food on the table. I know now how difficult it must have been for him to swallow his pride and go back to a team that he did not see as 'team' anymore. But what do you know, sometimes there are stronger forces working that push a man to go out of character.

To step out of a comfort zone. To change.

37

Portrait: Splendour on the grass

Shutter speed: 125; Aperture: 8; Available light (mid-afternoon); Top angle; Close-up; Sepia tone.

Out of the corner of my eye, I spotted her – this small, ragged, street urchin. She may have only been ten... or even nine.

She saw me fussing with my SLR camera as I crouched to get the right shot of the main minaret of the old museum building. That was my chosen subject for my university photo language assignment.

Had she finished scrounging for her day's earnings? Was she working in a group? Was she hoping I'd part with some cash?

I ignored her for a good five minutes as she hopped,

skipped and tossed about on the grass... all the time giving my camera a sideways glance.

Satisfied that I had all the possible shots I needed of the museum façade and minaret, I started packing up to move on.

That's when she bounced up to me and without a word motioned for me to take her photograph. I was already running late. My classmates had already wrapped up and were waiting across the street. But her direct, open gaze meant that I just couldn't refuse her.

I nodded and she immediately prepared herself, squatting on the grass a few metres ahead, sweeping her short, dark hair back, smoothing down her worn-out skirt and looking up as I tip-toed to get a good top angle.

She didn't smile. She didn't pose. She just looked up – still, silent, artless.

I took one shot. And she jumped up to my side to see. But it was an old manual SLR, with no LCD screen to display images taken. I told her as simply as I could that there was no way to see how it had come out. She nodded. She did not understand. But she understood.

My friends called out from across the street.

I pulled out my wallet quickly to dig out some coins for my little subject. But she shook her head, smiled, and skipped away.

In the dark room that night, I ditched the museum as subject and went with the girl.

I received my teacher's scoring of the assignment a couple of days later. "Excessive light in the background," he remarked. "Distracts from the subject. A smaller aperture would have helped."

38

For the good times

Uncle Cliff was incorrigible.

There was no opportunity that he let pass to have a laugh – very often at some unsuspecting soul's expense. There were no subjects off limits. No outlandish pranks that seemed too extreme.

Everybody was fair game – His pious mother who took everything at face value, his younger siblings, and later on, his wife and children, his nephews and nieces, friends and strangers.

His gift was to see the delightful possibilities in the most mundane circumstances. To conjure up bizarre, but completely believable tales that left his listeners aghast... wondering if they were in the presence of a completely unhinged individual or a truly remarkable person. It wasn't unusual for him to break out into rhyme, song or complete gibberish... whatever the moment dictated.

He rode both the highs and lows of his career with mild bemusement. When he had much, he spread the love. When he hit a rough patch, he wielded a bittersweet sense of irony to giggle and cackle at fate.

It was not that he was delusional. His love of the fine things in life ensured that he bled when pricked. But as his nephews, we always suspected that a smile and a chortle were never far from his browbeaten gait when subdued by misfortune.

There was a time when – well past his active years – he found himself having to live temporarily in his younger brother's home. In debt, with no certainty of future income, no contact with his own grown children, and with no place to call his own, this old man still drew up wildly ambitious plans to rise from the ashes.

One afternoon, I saw him sitting cross-legged on the bed, taking a much-needed break from his incessant ramblings. He looked up as I entered the room and launched into it; quietly and in a warm, wonderful cadence: *"Don't look so sad. I know it's over. But life goes on. And this old world will keep on turning."*

In the next room, his brother heard and did what he could to stop the tears.

39

Into the woods

Decades ago, in that hazy dreamscape of childhood, I read Thoreau's '*Walden*' and resolved to do as he did. To leave the safety of civilised life and live alone in the woods, surviving – no, thriving – by sheer self-reliance and simple living. To pare down existence to the essentials. To introspect. To commune with nature. To "suck out all the marrow of life" as he put it.

But it turned out that life pulled a fast one and sucked the marrow right out of me instead! I hustled through university and early gains in my career. I got married. Ella and I had two kids. We stretched ourselves on the rack, just so we could have house, car, investments, and holidays.

But tucked away in some unlit corner was the longing to go back to basics. To strip down to a sublime solitude that could save.

So, one summer when the kids had gone to spend six weeks of their holidays with the grandparents, I told Ella that

I was going into the woods for a while. She knew this was coming. But never for once did she think I'd have the guts to follow through. I was no experienced hand at camps. I read little of the many 'survival' manuals at the library. I watched nothing of the assortment of 'surviving the wild' shows on TV. I'd never experienced anything close to an army boot camp. I was not even very athletic.

But my goal was to meet each new problem that the wild presented without the package of readymade solutions from others. Of course, I would go in with some tools... and putting that gear together occupied me for a week – axe, saw, knife, shovel, cooking pot, a few cups, plates, forks and spoons, a portable camping stove, a ferro rod and matches, water bottle, fishing rod with assorted hooks, toiletries, clothing, tent, sleeping bag, insect repellent, first aid kit, flashlight, and batteries.

All through the week, Ella kept checking to see if I was serious about the plan. As the week drew to a close, she became anxious that my resolve hadn't wavered.

The plan was for me to drive eight hours to reach the last rest area within Whitman's Wood, leave the car there and trek the rest of my way into the centre. I told Ella, I'd shoot for a one-month stay, but that I would extend if it was working well.

Whitman's Wood was the obvious choice since it had no known predators. It was fed by the fresh waters of Cathedral Springs where I could also fish for my supper and collect my daily supply of water. Best of all, there were parts of it not yet assaulted by campers, bird watchers, trekkers, and the holiday crowds.

I left as planned. I trekked as planned. And just when the light started fading, I found myself a good clearing to camp at for the first night. There was no need for a campfire – I skipped having to rustle up dinner by finishing up the last of the pasta that Ella had packed for me in the morning.

As I pitched my tent, the forest started waking up to a hot and humid night. Tucked into my sleeping bag and with the tent zipped shut, I listened to the chirping, buzzing, and thrumming of birds, crickets, and geckos. It was good to be alone with the forest.

I was close to drifting off to sleep when I heard it. The distinct sound of slithering past dried leaves just outside my tent. I stopped breathing and waited. Half a minute passed, and I heard it again. This time creeping closer to the tent.

In many of my discussions with Ella as I prepared, we spoke of storms... of insect bites... of parasites in freshwater... of stinging jellyfish.... of sunstroke... of sudden bushfires... but somehow the topic of snakes did not come up.

Now, in the dark of the forest, with a legless demon encircling my tent, I fought back morbid thoughts of what I would have to contend with if the freaking thing bit me –blurred vision, slurred speech, blistering, swelling, extreme pain, drooling, paralysis, respiratory arrest and... a lonely, un-dignified end.

24 hours later, Ella and I were studiously scooping out the last portions of ice cream from the tub between us as our favourite cooking show started playing on the TV.

"So, once again, tell me what really happened?"

"I've told you three times already Ella!"

"Tell me again."

"I just realised, lying there in the tent, in the dark, last night, that it was just so silly of me to be leaving you here all by yourself. My date with the forest can wait."

"Really!! And I thought it couldn't wait... that you just had to do it... that you've been wanting to do it all your life!!"

"Yes Ella. It is something I'll take a shot at some other time. Right now, I'm glad to be home with you. Aren't you?"

"Yes, I am... but... did something happen last night?"

"Nothing Ella... I just came to my senses; that's all. So, tell me, you reckon Team Blue is going to cop it this time from Gordon?"

40

Incomplete

He hated filling in forms.

They made him nervous and unsure of himself.

If anyone interrupted him while he was filling in a form, he became irritable and impatient with them.

But this was the mother of all forms – he was applying for a permanent resident visa.

Given that he was single, he thought it would be fairly simple.

But he had been at it for 20 minutes already and was still not sure he was making any progress.

Every time he had to go hunt for supporting documentation, his blood pressure shot through the roof. The problem was that it highlighted just how sloppy he was with keeping his certificates and documents in order.

They had questions on address history for the last ten years... travel movements for the last ten years... employment history... educational qualifications... it just went on and on! And if that wasn't enough, they also saw it fit to ask if he had pending convictions, was he a sex offender, was he charged with genocide, had he been involved in people smuggling, was he a threat to national security...

When he found himself stopping to scan through his past for any misdemeanours... when he saw himself taking these outrageous questions seriously – that was when something snapped in him.

He put down his pen, shut the file of forms and threw it into the bottom of a deep drawer.

He found those incomplete forms three decades later as he was cleaning up to downsize.

He smiled as he tossed the full folder into the bin.

"I doubt I'd have enjoyed that weather anyway". That was what he told those who asked him why he did not migrate.

41

Last tour over the reef

I reached Pollock Hospital 30 minutes early. ID check completed, they scanned and then rummaged through my handbag, confiscated my phone, conducted a pat-down search, and brought the sniffer dog in to check for concealed drugs. In the visitor zone, I was told to wait while they fetched their most celebrated inmate.

Lucian Healy appeared shorter than I expected.

"Thank you, Dr Healy. I know you must be getting so many of these requests from journalists."

"That's alright, Ms Alvarez. Gives me a chance to get away from some of the more unhinged inmates in my ward. Just fire away."

"So why don't we start at somewhere before your publication in 'Nature' that spectacularly demolished the whole coral reef protection approach as we knew it at the time?

"Okay. The science and its implications were simple

enough even for the politicians to get their head around – you have global warming, rising temperature levels in the oceans, disruption of the symbiotic relationship between coral reefs and microscopic algae, corals forced to expel the algae (and so lose their colour and their sustenance through photosynthesis), accelerated coral bleaching, eventual collapse of the reef system, reduction in the diversity of sea life, massive losses to fisheries and tourism that depend on the reefs, and higher risk of coastline damage in regions once protected by the reefs."

"Yes. And the scale of the 2016 Great Barrier Reef bleaching event reinforced the urgent need for decisive action."

"Not just in Australia. The global scale of the 2014-2017 coral bleaching events led the scientific community to a grim consensus – given that the world was past the tipping point in terms of global warming, the destruction of coral reefs in tropical seas was almost certain within a century."

"But this was before you, Dr Healy published your piece in 'Nature', with a model that suggested that thermal-stress and its implications on the reefs were grossly exaggerated."

"Yes. It had a seismic effect."

"But how Dr Healy? How did the whole world, the entire scientific community, governments, the multinationals, and the press take you seriously?

"You must remember that my paper just before that was unimpeachable – the one that identified huge variations in the degree of impact of rising sea-surface temperatures on coral reefs across regions and species. And that was based on hard evidence collected over two decades across literally thousands of sites globally."

"But your paper in 'Nature'... the model that demolished the idea that coral reef bleaching could be directly linked to rising sea-surface temperatures – that paper was based on no hard evidence."

"The model had been tested. But yes, there was no hard evidence."

"So basically, you made it all up?"

"I still think that I got some elements of the model right. Like the fact that some reefs had, over time, developed a certain degree of resilience that helped them handle thermal stress better than others."

"But Dr Healy. Your paper effectively cut the funding legs out from under conservation movements that were protecting the reefs."

"Yes. It did that."

"Half a century's worth of evidence-based research by your own peers was basically overturned overnight."

"Yes."

"And after that no one seemed to care that the genuine science-driven projects were without backers. After that, you became the poster boy for every climate-change skeptic in government."

"Yes."

"And the El-Nino that followed took out 95% of the coral reefs globally."

"Yes."

"Gone for good."

"Yes."

"And we could have done something about it if your fabricated findings had not distracted us all."

"You could say that."

"How did you make this most blatant lie so believable?"

"By the time I put out that paper, I was already attaining some sort of cult status in the scientific community, as a rebel with an oversized brain and scandalous ideas. And mind you even among the nameless, faceless citizen scientists who form the backbone of all the volunteer effort for the reefs, I was being seen as a sort of unsettling, but plausible reality check."

"So, the scientific community took your word for it?"

"Yes. The brilliance of the model's design and the audacious premise it was built on persuaded them that the inconsistencies in the data were just insignificant anomalies."

"And you are here now – probably the first scientist to be sentenced to life in prison for scientific misconduct and fraud.

"This isn't a prison Ms Alvarez... it's an asylum."

"For the criminally insane."

"Okay, you have a point there."

"This wasn't about selective or misleading use of data. This wasn't about any sloppiness in terms of analysis. This was a wrong conclusion arrived at in the full knowledge that it had no scientific basis... and the deliberate substantiation of such a conclusion through artful misrepresentation."

"The courts have been through all of this Ms Alvarez... I don't need reminders of what I have done."

And so, he continued.

I spent another hour listening to his meandering tale – an unremarkable childhood, early wins at university, a penchant for picking the most controversial stands on hotly debated environmental issues, the richly deserved accolades for his

early work on variations in impact of sea-surface temperatures. But nothing in all of that hinted at or explained that
one-off diabolical fabrication that eventually kicked the cli-
mate change movement between the legs. He wasn't personally for or against protection of the environment. In fact, the
more he spoke, the more I realised that he really did not seem
to have any genuine convictions on anything at all. He simply
enjoyed the power that came with using a very sharp mind to
shake up long held beliefs.

When I thought I'd got enough material for my piece, I
thanked him and stood up to leave.

He seemed reluctant to end it.

As I turned to the door, he smiled, threw up his hands
expansively and said, "All in all, Ms Alvarez, you've got to
at least admit that I managed to force every environmental
enthusiast and scientist to question findings on both sides of
the debate."

"No, Dr Healy. You did more than that. Let me tell you this:
As a teen, I was in a semi-submersible, touring the Great Barrier Reef. This must have been a couple of decades ago. And
I still carry that memory of such astounding beauty below
the surface. To think that such other-worldly magnificence
existed somewhere on this planet – regardless of whether we
humans acknowledged it or celebrated it – that was to be
consoled that all was not lost. But that magnificence... it no
longer exists. My child will never have that opportunity. You
took that away from her. Not because you believed in anything. That would have been forgivable. No, Dr Healy. You
do not get the pleasure of my hate or the world's hate. That

would be too good for you. All you get – unfortunately for you – is our plain disgust."

42

Hallowed ground

We had a big, framed image of the Sacred Heart of Jesus at home.

It rested on a dark wooden base and that was our altar.

The picture – in muted shades of brown, beige and red – was in a black frame.

Fortunately, Dad and Mum had the good sense not to clutter that altar with other distractions.

For some years it was bigger than us kids. But then we grew up.

We said our family prayers before it. We whispered quiet pleas for help in our school examinations. We asked for protection before a long road trip.

It was a lovely image.

Jesus looked down at us with his nail-pierced hands; open, welcoming. The flaming heart in his bosom bled from the cut of thorns. A small cross rested on his sacred heart.

There was a gentle sadness in his eyes.

43

A cyberattack gets personal

This is Police Officer Imran Wahab. And this is the story of the hardest arrest I've had to make in my entire career.

8:30 pm
So, what's going to happen now, Don?
Nothing.
What do you mean, nothing?
The decision is final, Mel. They will not change their mind.
But after all the years you've given to the company.
I know.
And you were not the only one. You were just the one who got caught.
I know.

Can we not get a lawyer to help? There should be some grounds for unfair dismissal?

Maybe.

So? Are you just going to sit there and take it?

No.

So, what are you going to do?

I'm going to bring this company to its knees.

You're going to do what? You are one control system operator against one of the largest water utilities in the country. I know you have some grand delusions. But for once, let's get real, Don.

You think I'm joking?

Okay Don. You're not joking. Now why don't I set out some dinner and we can talk of your plan then... that is if you have one.

Okay, Mel. I'll just be on my laptop for a bit... just call me when you're ready.

8:50 pm

Don, dinner's ready.

Coming.

I just rushed through Don.

Looks good Mel.

You have the fish... I had it this afternoon.

Okay.

So, what's your plan?

It's done.

What?

They are going to regret firing me the way they have.

What did you do?

15 minutes on the laptop was enough.

To do what?

To cripple the entire water network.

Okay, stop it, Don. You're getting me worried.

I just took down the entire control system of the eastern treatment plant and the central wastewater network.

You can do that?

Of course, I can, and I just did. It may be one of the largest water utilities in the country. But Mel, it has one of the most antiquated automation and control systems ever. This plant has system vulnerabilities everywhere you look. I only needed a remote wireless Internet connection and knowledge of which system patches were not updated to manipulate valve and flow operations.

And what would that have done?

That means very soon, the night shift at the plant is going to contend with a cocktail of sewage and drinking water mixed together!

You did not!

Yes, I did.

No, you did not!

Okay, don't believe me if you don't want to. But for an operator who has been at the plant for a good two decades, it's not that difficult to cripple the network remotely.

Let's say you did. Were you planning to send that soup through the drinking water supply to all our homes?

No, Mel. The alarm flood that would have been triggered would have got them to shut down the entire water supply in two minutes. I was not planning to spread disease and death through the city. Just bring the plant to a halt. Show them that they messed with the wrong guy.

Okay, for a moment there I thought you'd lost it completely! So, no sewage coming through the taps, right?

No, Mel. But there will be drinking water supply disruption tonight for sure. Till they clean up the mess.

Don, you really should not have gone that far!

We're talking about my entire career here, Mel! No one is going to be hiring me at my age.

6 am the next morning
Hello Don, this is Imran.

Hi Imran. You realise it's a bit early in the day to be calling up your mates?

Don, this is not the time for small talk.

What happened?

I'm coming over to your house in the next 15 minutes. I'm at the station now. But I'll be over with a couple of others.

What happened, Imran?

You tell me, Don. I got the call from the eastern treatment plant at 4 am. You tell me what happened when I get there.

Tell you what?

You thought you could just snoop into the control network and play games with the water supply?

They fired me last evening, Imran. I bet they didn't tell you that.

So? So, you did this?

I just gave them a scare, Imran. That's all it was. I fiddled with the system to stuff up the water supply just enough to shut down the plant. But I knew it would trigger the alarms soon enough for them to shut down supply before any real damage was done.

And you think we're going to believe that story, Don? I've known you for three decades. Don't tell me that. You remember, you are talking to a Police Officer. It's not Friday night drinks, Don.

It's the truth, Imran. I just wanted to send them a strong message. That's all.

Yes, strong enough I'd say. Nausea, vomiting, abdominal pain, cramps, diarrhoea, burning throats – the hospital has been flooded with over 80 patients over the last four hours who drank your vile cocktail.

What! I didn't do that. I told you, I just...

You opened up the fluoride injector pump, Don. Did you really have to do that? Your superintendent at the plant tells me the average fluoride level is one part per million. Do you know what the levels were after your little game? 225 parts per million.

Oh my God! I thought I'd just fiddled with the wastewater line valves!!

I'm calling you as a courtesy Don. Get dressed and stay put. We'll be over in 15 minutes. And we're taking you back to the station.

Imran!! I swear I didn't mean to...

And Don, I don't know how to say this. The fluoride spike resulted in three fatalities overnight – dialysis patients at the hospital. Of all the nights for it to happen, the system used to filter fluoride out of the tap water for dialysis failed last night. It had been giving some trouble on and off. But this fluoride spike was too much for it to handle. Three patients suffered massive heart failure and could not be revived. One of them was... I hope Mel is around to be with you till we come..

Who Imran?

One of them was your mum, Don. I'm so sorry. I truly am. Now put Mel on the phone so I can speak to her.

44

At the lake

It was work-from-home Tuesday.

I opened the door to our balcony and stepped out with a mug of hot tea.

It was going to be another lovely, sun-drenched morning.

There were already a number of early morning walkers and joggers around our lake.

Most preferred to park their cars on the street – bumper to bumper – just opposite our balcony. So, I was afforded an undisturbed view of every family getting their morning workout.

A young man – probably in his thirties – got into his car after his jog. But instead of pulling out and driving off, he opened his glove compartment, pulled out a small piece of paper and scribbled a note. He then got out of his car, walked to the car parked just behind him and placed his note under the front windscreen wiper.

I stopped sipping my tea.

Without a pause, he headed back to his vehicle and drove off.

Had he accidentally hit or dented the car behind him? Was his note a brief apology with contact phone number?

I didn't have long to wait.

A young lady walked back to her car a couple of minutes later... the same car with the note on the windscreen.

She didn't notice it till she had got in and strapped up. She paused a second... unbuckled, stepped out and pulled the paper from under the wiper.

I waited.

She read it quickly and headed straight back into her car.

What was happening? Didn't she want to survey the damage he'd caused? Was it a mere scratch or an ugly dent?

Before I could resolve the question, she drove off!

She simply read a strange note left on her windscreen... and left!

If he hadn't backed into her car and hit it, what was that note about?

If it wasn't a pamphlet marketing some local business – I know it wasn't – then what was the unspoken message from one to the other?

The pair didn't look like spies... although I haven't seen any in the flesh.

They didn't look like secret lovers fixing up their next rendezvous.

They didn't even look like an actual couple who had arrived in different cars – with him just reminding her to pick up the milk on her way back home!

I went back into the kitchen.

The last zoom call for the day was our team wellbeing meeting. The question to be answered – 'Share with the team something that has been bothering you lately'.

David, my boss spoke passionately about the huge delta in our sales numbers and how that kept him awake at night. Louise spoke about the frustration of not being able to see her extended family during the lockdown, especially given her father's declining health. Wilhelm spoke about the frustration about having to wait for the second dose of the vaccine. Andre, one of our interns spoke about how rude a client had been with him during a call that morning.

And then, my turn.

"Oh, nothing that's really bothering me," I began. "But maybe one of you can help me here. This morning, just at the lake near our house…"

45

Glaring mistakes

His wife's arthritic fingers had started playing up. So, he asked his grown son to type out the presentation text that had to go up on the overhead projector for the next lesson.

For weeks, his son promised to get it done, but never did.

The night before the class, with a hint of mild exasperation in his voice, he asked his son if he was going to get round to it. The dour faced young man stared moodily at his father, but finally shuffled off reluctantly to the desktop computer.

The next day, the students murmured gleefully that the professor's presentation was riddled with spelling errors and formatting glitches. So uncharacteristic of him!

For a man who prided himself on his professionalism, it was hard to swallow.

46

Final memo

Dear Team,

Some of you may already know. But not all.

And I realise that those that do are still not sure that I'm serious.

So, to make myself absolutely clear, I sent in my letter of resignation to our Board of Directors last night. I have officially stepped down as CEO.

Kim (now hasn't she been just terrific as our CFO for these last two years!) will take over with immediate effect as CEO. You are in good hands.

At the Board's request, I've agreed to remain available for a few strategic negotiations with a couple of our key accounts over the next two months. But beyond that, it's pretty much a clean break.

As soon as our kids finish the school year, Yuja and I plan to transition back to our house in the country. So, I'm not going to the competition across the street. And I'm not taking up another similar role anywhere.

To many of you, this may come as a surprise. I'm sure there are a number of questions you may want answered.

Are we in trouble? No, this is not the case of the captain abandoning the sinking ship. On the contrary, we have never done better in our two decades as a company. We continue to win large and long-term contracts, grow our share of the market, expand our geographic footprint, and attract the best talent.

Are we going to be in trouble? No, there isn't some up-coming investigation or scandal that was going to have com-promised my role. I'm not leaving to pre-empt being kicked out. And our Board has never doubted or second-guessed me in any of our major transformation decisions.

Am I in trouble? No, I haven't been diagnosed with a terminal illness that is forcing me to reset. I'm hoping that I can continue to make meaningful contributions wherever the road takes me. But yes, there's something that's changed.

You have been family to Yuja, the kids and to me all these years. And so, I'm taking the liberty of sharing with you some personal thoughts that might explain this sudden decision.

Last week, I unearthed a letter that my mother had writ-ten to our kids almost a year ago. It wasn't a list of dos and don'ts to her grandchildren. It wasn't a how-to manual. It wasn't even sage advice on what makes a good life.

In her letter, my mother spoke of her childhood without toys. Not because she could not have them. But because she had so much else to fill her day. Living in a house only a couple of yards from the river, hers was a home infused with the sights and sounds of nature. At the time, she was still the only child, but her playmates were her dog, the chickens, turkeys, ducks, even the pigeons that came to feed off the rice bran scattered out for them. She watered, weeded, and pruned the small vegetable patch that they had near the well and the beds of flowering plants in the garden. She spent hours on the swing tied to a mango tree amidst the coconut trees. She named the birds. She watched out for hatching chicks. She introduced ducklings to the water. She played peacemaker when her boisterous dog chased the birds. She even looked out for seals coming out of the river to rest.

I'm not sure what her grandchildren thought of it, but that simple recount of a life on the land unsettled me. Perhaps the two decades of unrelenting pressure to grow our company had shifted some tectonic plates inside me. Perhaps it was only a matter of time before I felt the tremors.

Moments of insight come to us unbidden. I don't know why, but that letter made me revisit every certainty I had about my life to now. Perhaps who I thought I should be was completely different to who I could be. That may sound mawkish. But sometimes the sentimental does the impossible. As you've heard me say time and again, emotion brings energy.

I do not discount the passion and the perseverance that brought me fulfilment in the corporate world. Not for one minute do I retract all my exhortations to each of you to make the goals of our company your own. But when you crack ice, there's no telling which way the fissures will run.

You will recall the catchphrase that I made our unofficial company motto – "Success is good. Significance is better."

May each of you continue to find significance in your work and in your lives, even as I rediscover where mine must lie.

Goodbye and God bless.

47

Beethoven reviews Brahms

For a few hours last winter, I played host to the strangest house guest ever.

Let me recount this weird and wonderful story as plainly as I can.

As a child, air-conducting feverishly before our home sound system, with Messrs Tchaikovsky, Karajan, and the Berlin Philharmonic at my service, I assumed that I was destined to mount podiums in every major concert hall as a revered maestro of the classical music world. But I soon discovered that conducting was more than waving arms in dramatic fashion. You actually had to do the blasted music theory.

But I digress. The point I was trying to make is that among the pantheon of great composers, Ludwig van has been to me the summit of all art. His symphonies, sonatas, quartets, and concertos are for me the kernel of aesthetic experience. In other words, these transcendent works kill it like nothing else can.

Of course, there are smaller altars built to Bach and Mozart, and the others. But in my scheme, the cathedral belongs to Herr Beethoven.

It was not only about his superhuman courage in the face of deafness, illness, and isolation. The music was simply so bloody incandescent.

I remember heading into tough days, humming the first movement theme of his *Eroica Symphony* to myself, and feeling new strength return. I recall being thrown every time I heard that mighty upward rush of the strings at the climax of his *Overture Leonore III*. The ethereal stasis of the 'Hymn of Thanksgiving' from his *String Quartet Opus 132*... the sublime autumnal musing of the *Larghetto* from his *Violin Concerto*... the hallowed world of the *Benedictus* from his *Missa Solemnis*... that transfigured ending of his final piano sonata... Okay, I shall desist from needless detours and get back to the story.

One chilly Sunday morning, I came home with some groceries to find a stranger asleep on the sofa! How he got there with the door still locked was beyond me. My surprise turned to incredulity when the gentleman in question roused himself from a deep slumber, sat up and scowled at me as if I was the intruder. That scowl! There was no mistaking it. Here in my living room was Ludwig van Beethoven!

I let the grocery bags drop to the floor, took three steps back, a tentative step forward, and let out the most unconvincing "Ahhh!"

The stern look on his face softened and he asked, "Where am I?"

"Beethoven?" I asked and exclaimed – both in the one word. I was still some way off from volunteering street address and postcode.

He answered. "Yes I am... but where am I?"

"You can't be" I offered. "This is 2019 and you died in 1827."

"I know", he said calmly.

"THE Beethoven?"

"Yes, I think my view on that is well documented. There is only one Beethoven."

"Yes... yes... I know" I gargled. "But freakin hell... Beethoven!!!"

"I'm permitted a brief return to see what has changed."

"Slow down... you are permitted by who?"

"They gave me a few hours... that's all."

"Is this for real? For one, you died stone deaf... and here you are holding a completely normal conversation with me... and in English!!"

"When you reach the other bank, all limitations fall away."

"So, you can hear?"

"Yes, I can."

"You are real?"

"Yes, I am."

Half a minute of silence followed.

"Beethoven, before this dream ends, I... I just wanted to say thank you... for all that you've given me in your music. All that you've given the world."

My voice cracked... this was too much for me to handle at the end of a routine grocery run.

He smiled.

And it struck me that I was now the only person alive in the whole world to have seen Beethoven without his trademark scowl or glare. Painters and sculptors seemed to have transmuted his mighty genius into a perpetually stern and angry frown... forever at war with people and his fate. But his genuine pleasure on hearing my gushing appreciation of his work confirmed to me that history had completely missed the point – he was a composer who responded to tragedy with unbridled joy and hope (and eventual acceptance).

His deep-set eyes looked over my living room.

He stood up.

At 5 feet 5 inches, he was no taller than me... but I was quaking at the knees. Here before me was the man who redefined the role of the artist. Here in flesh and blood was the one who revolutionised music and imbibed it with a spirituality that still resonates. Here in the 21st century, by some twisted time-jumping fantasy, was the Shakespeare of music, in conversation with one of his star-struck devotees.

"Can I get you something?" I asked.

"Yes, I need your help."

"Anything Mr Beethoven... anything... just tell me."

"I don't have long. So, can I listen to some of my late works? The music upstairs is infinitely better, but I missed hearing most of my last works."

"You don't say!! The music is better up there?"

"No comparison."

I lurched towards the nearest chair and sat down. Too much new information for one morning. This was getting patently mind-bending.

Okay, late works.

I quickly sat the master down in front of the wide-screen TV, explained to him that with the magnificent strides mankind had made in technology, we could now see and hear performances right in our homes without the need for heading to the concert hall. I then played back-to-back DVDs of Barenboim's performance of the last piano sonata, Karajan and the Berlin Philharmonic's performance of the *Missa Solemnis* and the *Ninth Symphony*, and Bernstein and the Vienna Philharmonic's orchestral performance of the *String Quartet Opus 131*.

To see the master listen to his own last works – performed by arguably the finest interpreters on the planet – and to see how visibly moved he was by the experience – that will always remain one of the peak experiences of my little life.

As he listened in silence, tears streamed down his face.

Not wanting to break the spell, I left him by himself to soak in the experience and went into my spare bedroom. I located the box of music scores that I had stashed away and pulled out a few that I wanted to show him.

When the music stopped, I brought him those scores.

"Mr Beethoven, I don't know if you realise it, but your legacy extends way past your own music. It has transformed the thinking and work of every composer since. I took the liberty of bringing you some scores of your successors – just so you can see for yourself the amazing possibilities you helped create for all who followed you."

His eyes lit up like a child and he gratefully grabbed the stack I handed him and pored over them closely.

I excused myself and stepped out of the room to rustle up some food for my guest.

I came back to the living room in half an hour.

And he was gone.

I looked through every room in the apartment. He was really gone. Just like that. Just as suddenly as he had appeared to me.

I dropped into the sofa that he had just been sitting in and let it all sink in.

And then it struck me. I had not thought to take a quick picture or brief video of him on my mobile phone. That way, the world would know that I was not some demented freak with a wild imagination. That way, the world would know that Beethoven was here.

My head in my hands, I rued the colossal, missed opportunity. And then I spotted them. The scores that I had handed him lay scattered on the sofa. I saw unsteady scrawls on some of them. On the score of Schubert's *'Unfinished' Symphony*, he'd written simply, "Sublime!" On the score of Chopin's *Nocturnes* and *Preludes*, "Genius!" And finally, on the score of Brahms' *Fourth Symphony*, "This here is my successor!"

The next day at the office, Ben spoke at length about his son's weekend football game. Clara told us of a new Portuguese restaurant that she had discovered. Rajiv talked up the movie premiere that he'd been to. And then, turning to me, he asked, "So what were you up to on the weekend?"

48

The view from base camp

He reached the foot of the hill and realised that he would not make it to the top.

He had forgotten to bring his inhaler.

Should he jog back to the hotel?

No. That would mean he would be too late to catch the last of the sunset.

He would just have to do without it.

As he hurried up what was initially a gentle ascent, he began to feel the strain in his breath.

He had just a few minutes before the sun set.

He pushed on.

There is not much you can do when you deal with an asthma attack except conserve your breath. Make it count.

But as he clambered up the rocky pathway cut into the hill, conserving his breath was the last thing he could do.

Quickening his pace, he felt his chest heave in ragged protest, his heart pound faster, the sweat pour freely.

The light was losing its brilliance.

His scrambled steps were not going to get him to the top in time.

He turned the next steep bend and found a flat rock that overlooked the silent valley.

He sat down and gazed out.

He did not make the summit, but the view from this base camp would have to do. He looked on as that fiery eternal orb dipped into the murky distant horizon and disappeared in an instant.

The valley slipped into shadow as he gasped and heard the whistling of his lungs harmonise with the faint breeze humming through the trees.

49

First warning

So, what's with your Pope?

What about him?

Is he still in hiding?

Yes. But I'm sure you did not haul me out of my workday to discuss the whereabouts of the Pope. I don't think I can help you there.

Of course, you can't. I know that. What I wanted to discuss with you, Mr Stern was more around your own whereabouts last Sunday, the 9th.

And why would that be of interest, may I ask?

So where were you at 9.30 am on the Sunday?

Officer, I'm not sure that it is any of your business. Am I being charged with any crime? I'd really like to know.

If you've got nothing to worry about, then just answer the question. Where were you at 9.30 am last Sunday?

At a friend's house.

Who and where?

Maxim McGrath. 13 Torrens Court, Wattle Grove.

And what was the purpose of your visit?

I told you, he is a friend.

And what was the purpose of your visit?

We just dropped in for a leisurely Sunday breakfast.

When you say 'we', who else was with you?

My wife and our two kids.

Okay. And who else was there?

A number of other friends known to both Maxim and to me.

Oh, so it was a gathering?

I wouldn't call it that.

How long did you stay?

A couple of hours, I suppose.

Okay. I'll let you in on a little secret. We have Maxim in the next room, and he's already confessed to holding a religious gathering on the same day, same time, same place that you say you were having this leisurely Sunday breakfast.

We did have breakfast.

I'm sure you did. But that was not why you were there. Was it?

Alright, we did have breakfast after a prayer session.

Aha! Now we're getting somewhere!

Why should anyone have a problem with that?

I believe that gathering was an unregistered group.

I met up with some friends and we had a prayer meeting. Why would I have to worry about registered or unregistered?

It was a gathering of over 25 people, Mr Stern.

Officer, I really did not count. I'm sure Maxim – in the next room – has already told you how many were there.

Yes, he has, Mr Stern and he is extremely regretful that he omitted to register the group with the Department Against False Gods.

Last I heard, that Department was against all Gods!

Mr Stern. No need for sarcasm. We are trying to be helpful here.

In what way?

I was coming to that. Were your children in attendance at this prayer session?

They were not required to be, but yes, they came in from the backyard and sat with us during the session.

Mr Stern! Don't you realise that you are entering dangerous territory, here?

I'm sorry, I really do not understand what this has to do with you or anybody else?

Mr Stern! Your children are 8- and 10-years young! Is it responsible parenting indoctrinating them with myths and untruths when they do not yet have the faculties to make up their own minds?

I cannot believe this! Do the police have anything better to do than to spy on what I do with my children?

Mr Stern, I'm sure you are familiar with the 'right to reality' principles that our President has been championing with untiring devotion.

I've nothing to say about that.

Mr Stern, we as a society have moved on from primitive practices based on unsubstantiated beliefs. The 'right to reality' principle is unambiguous – it is not real if it is not proven by science.

Officer, I really am not interested in debating this with you.

But, your children, Mr Stern! Your irrational affiliation is corrupting their thinking. How do you expect our education system to cope with students who are fed a diet of untruths at home? Don't you realise that religious beliefs are incompatible with the vision of a truly enlightened society that our President wishes for us?

And what about freedom? Why aren't we talking about the freedom to choose what we believe in?

Precisely, Mr Stern! That is what I am getting at. Your children should be given the freedom to choose. Instead, you are attempting to force-feed them with lies and that is tantamount to dissent against the State.

Officer, I'm asking you again. Have I been charged with a crime?

No, Mr Stern. Not yet.

Then I'm leaving if that's alright with you.

Of course, Mr Stern. But please do exercise a bit more restraint in the future when it comes to matters such as these. You were once in the majority, Mr Stern. But not anymore. Our children must not be robbed of their inalienable right to reality.

You mean my children.

Yes, your children, in this case.

And you mean the right to only a visible and tangible reality.

A science-based reality, Mr Stern. Which is the ONLY

reality there is. On that there is no other view that can be accepted.

And what's to happen with Maxim in the next room?

You need not concern yourself with him, Mr Stern. He will be given ample time to think through the consequences of organising an unregistered religious gathering.

How much 'time', officer?

Let's just say, you won't be seeing him till after the next New Year's celebrations. Drive safe, Mr Stern.

50

King of the road

Uncle Elmore was many things to us. Warm. Affable. Generous. He was also the first hard-core motorbike enthusiast that I ever knew. And the object of his affections was not just any bike. It was a black Enfield Bullet 350 cc.

The first Bullet rolled out in 1932. By the 1980s, when Uncle Elmore had returned to India from the Middle East and owned one, it had already attained a cult following in the country. With its unmistakable thump and its imposing build, it had for decades been the favoured ride for the Indian army and the police.

To Uncle Elmore, it was more than an iconic motorbike. It was a statement. Not a brash 'look-at-me' statement that faster, lighter, and more contemporary bikes shouted. That would have been so out of character with the Bullet.

Cast iron engine, large teardrop fuel tank, spring supported saddle seat, telescopic fork suspension in front, sizable twin shock absorbers at the rear, foot operated gear change, chrome detailing – the Bullet was the quintessential cruiser.

On it, you could never hope to power past 110 kilometres per hour. But no hard-core Bullet enthusiast would ever have wanted to hurry on such a ride.

You could certainly not expect great things in terms of fuel efficiency.

And yet, with hardly any advertising worth the name, with little real change in the model for decades, the Bullet became a revered marquee in the two-wheeler world.

I recall Uncle Elmore leaning back on his imposing ride, feeling like the king of the road.

I recall him sitting my eight-year-old younger brother on the hefty fuel tank and letting him take control of the Bullet for a few seconds as they rode sedately down a quiet side street one Sunday afternoon.

But the most vivid memory remains that of the weekends when we'd visit Uncle to find him stripping and cleaning his Bullet in the front yard. To see the man obsess about his bike was to see a quiet, wonderful passion find its own reward. Wiping dust and mud off wheel spokes, rims, and silencer... cleaning and lubricating the chain... tightening the nuts and bolts of the engine exhaust and silencer... cleaning the air filter... washing, polishing, and waxing the metal parts.

I'm not sure he needed to do it as frequently or as thoroughly as he did. But he did.

At that time, Uncle Elmore was grappling with an unexpected separation, a strained relationship with his ageing parents and his siblings, inexplicable health scares, and an uncertain future in terms of his career.

But the sight of this man-child hosing down his beloved Bullet on his sunlit front yard remains a memory that lingers.

They told us that the end was sudden. Still in his early forties, he collapsed while riding. And died of a cardiac arrest. Only, he wasn't on his Bullet, but on his bicycle.

These days, every time I see a muscle bike roar past, I think of Uncle Elmore and his Bullet.

51

Disturbing dreams

I dreamt that the sound guys were taking too long to sort out the microphones, and the audience lost interest even before we had a chance to perform. They started walking off even as we stood silent, helpless, and ready on stage.

I dreamt that the brakes wouldn't work, and the car just kept rolling downhill with no way for me to stop the crash.

Another time, I dreamt I was again at the wheel, but could not keep my eyes open. And I was too far gone to be able to slow or stop the car. The dark fog of sleep just refused to rise even as I struggled frantically to rouse myself up.

I dreamt that all my teeth came loose at the same time... and there was the distinct possibility of me becoming completely toothless.

I dreamt that I was certainly going to miss my flight.

I dreamt I was hanging off the ledge of a building... and slowly, but surely, losing my grip.

I dreamt of being caught in a mob.
I dreamt that I was in endless freefall.

And I dreamt that I could no longer wake from my dream.

52

A dog walks into
a bar - 1

A dog walks into a bar and asks the bartender for a low-calorie beer.

The bartender hesitates for a second and then serves him his drink.

The dog pretends not to notice, downs the beer, and then asks, "Why did you hesitate, Mr Bartender? Was there a problem?"

"No, sir," says the bartender, smiling weakly. "For a moment there, I mistook you for a French Bulldog. But I quickly realised that you're a Boston Terrier. So, as I said, no problem at all. We just don't serve French Bulldogs here."

53

Holy guacamole!

I knew a doctor who had a gift for detecting life-threatening disease just by sight.

Not sure how much of it was down to medical knowledge... because there is clearly an extensive body of research behind it. You know what I'm talking about, right? Asymmetric face, new moles, blotches, paleness, discolouration of the skin, hair loss, weight loss, shortness of breath, rashes, puffy or tired eyes, nail colour... there are so many visual cues that doctors use to validate diagnosis without touching the patient or doing any tests.

But this guy... he was bloody uncanny. A patient would walk in and even before he or she began speaking, our good doctor would go, "Holy guacamole!" That was it. The nurse in attendance would immediately jump into action. And before long, our patient would be in the ICU wondering how on earth that doctor knew that a stroke was imminent!

You may think detecting a stroke is straightforward, eh? What about the time he went "Holy guacamole!" and it was advanced cancer of the liver. Or another time it was an inoperable brain tumour. Or even difficult to diagnose conditions like Huntington's disease or fibromyalgia. He not only knew instantly when a patient was in mortal danger, but also what the exact cause was.

He did get into trouble a number of times for fast-tracking treatment programmes for some of his patients without waiting for scans and blood test results to come through. But that was only with the Medical Board. Never with his patients. A number of them owed their lives to his extraordinary ability to see the approaching shadow of death long before it was evident to others. Some were lucky in that there was still time to do something about it. Others not so. And yet even those unlucky ones thanked him for giving them the only heads-up that mattered.

I never knew him personally, but only heard about him from the junior doctors who worked with him at the hospital. One of them even asked him why it always had to be "guacamole" and not "Holy crap!" or "Holy cow!" or any other alternate curse word. Apparently, he hated guacamole; that's why.

After hearing about him for so many years, I finally rang him up to schedule a meeting with him on my way back from a medical conference that was a month away.

I thought nothing of it till I finished at the conference. But when I did turn up at his clinic, his trusted nurse apologised profusely for not having informed me earlier.

A week ago, the good doctor had looked in the mirror and uttered his last "Holy guacamole!"

54

It will soon get dark

I wake to find myself tied to a rock on a beach.

No one in sight.

It is just me, the chain, the rock... and the waves.

Each time the tide rises, I am swamped under. I struggle to free myself. But the chain is immovable. My chest is about to burst. I am seconds away from drowning. And just then, the tide recedes.

What joy! What relief! I gasp, gulp, giggle, and believe that it has ended.

But it hasn't.

I am still tied to the rock. And the next wave is building up to crash over me.

The light is fading... and it will soon get dark.

55

The Sandpiper's sacrifice

Mid-September... somewhere above the frozen mountains of Ecuador.

Arturo is terrified.

He is hurtling down with the other sandpipers... and there are no plans to pull away at the last.

"Mother!" Arturo screams – his call barely heard over the loud swoosh of the entire flock of birds dropping like dead weight through the clouds.

"It will be over soon, Arturo," his mother calls back.

"But why? Why?"

Against a mild breeze, the mother sandpiper drops closer to her terrified child. "It is what we do, Arturo."

"You mean we flew all the way from Alaska to Argentina and back up to Ecuador... just to suddenly stop flapping our wings and drop to our deaths here?"

"We sandpipers have been doing this every year... for generations, Arturo."

"But why, Mother? I don't want to die! If we are hungry, let's eat. If we are tired, let's rest our wings. We don't just give up and die like this!"

But the flock keeps hurtling down to the cold silent lagoons below.

The locals gather round the edge of the waters. Old and young agree that it is a surreal sight.

Up in the sky, just above the trees – "We are in this together, Arturo."

"Are we sick? Are we mad?"

"No Arturo. We are just pilgrims. In a few moments, when you hit the cold waters, your beating heart will be stilled... as will mine. But our journey does not end."

"This is not happening! This is not real!"

"Look at the humans looking up at us, Arturo! Look before it's too late. It is this sacrifice that tells them to carry on. But remember, we are no legend. This sacrifice is real. This death is real."

"Mother!"

"Goodbye my Arturo!"

"Mother!"

The flock hit the icy lagoons headfirst.

The locals wait and collect the washed-up bodies of the little fallen angels.

They celebrate the day as one of collective cleansing – with song and dance... and a delicious stew of sandpipers.

56

Your move

So, you want to take the bathtub out?

Yes.

And put in a new one?

No.

So, just get rid of it?

Yes.

You don't use it now?

No.

No time for a leisurely hour or two in the tub, eh?

No.

You know, when you sell the house, buyers will hope to see a bathtub in the bathroom.

I'm not selling the house.

No bathtub... that's a turn off for a buyer.

I'm not selling the house.

Sure... but when you do.

I'm not selling the house.

Whatever you say... It's just that if I was buying this house, I'd want a bathtub in.

How much to get that thing out of here?

It's not that simple.

Why?

You will have to replace cracked tiles around the tub and tile over the space where the tub was. And that won't match the rest of the floor tiles for sure. That means a full floor tiling of the bathroom.

Really?

And the bathroom has done its time...so I'll have to check the waterproofing underneath as well.

Really!

And when you pull out the tub, the wall over there is going to need a replaster and repaint... which will mean a new coat of paint for all the bathroom walls.

Uh...huh.

And your vanity and shower recess look dated – they're never going to match the new tiles. So, the question is do you want to take this opportunity to renovate the whole bathroom?

I just want that tub out of there.

Like I said...

57

Left for dead

This afternoon, for the first time in almost a year, someone stopped to look at me.

He was a teenager walking past on the other side of the street with his friends. They called him Josh.

Out of the corner of his eye, he spotted me in my yard and stopped in his tracks.

"Wow, look at that!!"

"Look at what?" his friends asked, almost in unison.

"That!"

"What?"

"That car, you idiots!"

"You mean that wreck?"

"Yes, that's a Chrysler Airflow."

"Get outta here... you actually know stuff like that?"

"Yes... that's certainly a Chrysler Airflow... from the 1930s."

"It's missing all tyres... there's not much of paint left on it... no window glass... it's pretty much a shell held together in cobwebs... in case you didn't notice, nerd."

"Don't say that!" Josh responded. "It was once something!"

"And we are sure you are going to enlighten us."

"You know what guys? If you talk about sales, this car was a disaster for Chrysler. But that was because its design was so far ahead of its time. Before the Airflow, cars were so aerodynamically inefficient, it was not funny. But with the Airflow, Chrysler cut out the drag – they designed a low and sleek vehicle – they did wind tunnel tests to design this – the first time ever for commercial car design... anywhere! No more the stodgy and boxy look. This was tapered rear and sloping nose! They also improved weight distribution by pushing the engine forward and relocating the rear seat down and forward, instead of its perch above the rear axle. They threw out the wooden frame bodies and went light-weight steel. Extended front and rear springs. Better safety and strength. Better handling. A far more comfortable ride than ever before. Also, more cabin space."

"So, what happened? Why did it fail?"

"Customers were just not ready for something that ground-breaking. I guess."

"Cool... let's take a selfie with your find, Josh."

The friends laughed, took their selfie with me, and hurried off.

As they turned the corner at the end of the street, Josh turned and looked back at me one last time.

His friends were right... I was now a shell held together by cobwebs. But Josh was also right – I was once something!

58

Eyewitness

So, what did the officer tell you?

He told me that you identified the suspect and gave him enough of an eyewitness testimonial to make this an open and shut case.

Come on inside, Sean. It's cold outside. Did you forget something?

I'll come to that in a moment. But Mother, can I ask you something?

What?

You told the officer that the person you saw on our street was the Gibson boy from our church?

Yes, the very same Cullen Gibson! Have they picked him up yet?

You stood on our front porch and saw him king hit the old man from behind?

Yes, that's what happened.

And this happened just after I left the house?

Yes, a half an hour ago. Otherwise, you would have seen what I saw.

That's true.

What's the matter, Sean?

And the officer said that you were certain it was Cullen and no one else?

Of course, it was!

And you are confident?

Sean, I might be old. But I'm not old and crazy!

I know you're not, mother. But isn't Cullen the guy that you've reported to the parish priest for disorderly conduct before?

The same rotten rogue!

Isn't he the same guy you kicked out of the fundraising carnival for not being 'Christian' enough?

He's a twisted troublemaker, Sean. He has no place in our community.

And you saw this same twisted fellow commit this crime on our street... a crime that could land him in jail for a good part of a decade?

A decade would be too little for that kind of fellow!

Mother! This is not only embarrassing... it's unnerving!

What?

I'm taking you to the police station right away so you can retract your statement.

You are going to what?

You heard me.

And why would I do that? Why would I let that scoundrel get away the one time I've caught him red-handed?

Because mother, I was coming back to give you your glasses. I mistakenly took your pair when I left the house... thinking it was mine when, all along, I had my own pair in my pocket.

But Sean...

And you and I know that you cannot tell the difference between a bloody tree and a human being from even five yards away without your glasses!!

59

Disinterested teenager listens as old man in a wheelchair holds forth at a loud party

How young are you?
Seventeen, sir.
I was seventeen not too long ago, you know.
Ha! Funny!
No, but seriously, you are the right age.
Right age for what?
To hear it.
To hear what?
The call to rapture.
And what's that?

There is a call to rapture, son. But it asks that a price be paid.

Sorry, can you repeat that? The music is too loud... I didn't get all of that.

I said, there is a call to rapture. But it asks that a price be paid.

What price?

To draw toward it, we must draw away from other things. And that choice we make not once and for all. But in every day. Every hour.

Uhmm?

The danger is not that we are indifferent. The danger is that we are too sensible. Too comfortable. Too knotted and too tangled to soar.

So, how do you answer this call to rapture?

We need two things. We need to know who we take along with us into the 'pathless woods' (as Byron called it). You've read Byron?

No.

Pathless woods – Do we go there alone – as some do? Do we go there alone some of the time – as most do? Do we go there with another?

Going with another gets complicated, right?

That depends.

On what?

The question is – are your important relationships the ties that bind or those that let you soar?

Uh-huh.

Second, you need to rekindle the embers. If you answer the call to rapture, you are not going to be without collateral damage. Passion cannot tiptoe quietly past. It leaves its mark. So, brace yourself for the firestorm.

Do you always talk like this? Or is it only after your second or third drink?

60

The last straw

What did you say?

I said, "You should be happy I've not cut your pay." These are tough times for all of us.

That's it.

That's what?

I'm out of here.

You are what?

You know Stan, you must think I'm some sort of an inanimate object.

I beg your pardon! I don't like your tone.

You won't be hearing much more of it for sure, Stan. I'm leaving.

You will do no such thing!

And what? You are going to get off your blasted wheelchair and stop me?

Where's this going? Are you upset about something?

No Stan. I'm not upset when you behave like a conceited bastard.

You are forgetting your place, now!

I'm not upset when you are hypercritical... obstinate... manipulative... insecure. I'm not upset when you cannot – even for a second – acknowledge that you may have something to do with your world being so out of joint.

Stop it!

Forget a log, you cannot accept that you've got half the Amazon Forest in your eye!

If I am all that, how come you put up with me so long?

It's a tough gig, Stan... but I have always reminded myself that you must have some good in you... in some quiet corner you wouldn't think to look in.

And, you are sure?

Have you seen the way your dog looks at you?

Ha! Very funny!

But it's just come to me as an epiphany, Stan.

What?

That it's a stupid dog. That it cannot tell a blighted bigot from a decent human being.

I have employed you for eight years! Does that count for nothing?

I have put up with you for eight years! Looked after you for eight years! That does count for something.

Don't come back to me when you cannot find work!

Oh, you sick, sorry, old windbag! You are estranged from your own children and grandchildren. You ignore every peace offering from them, even though it should be you saying 'sorry'. You have no friends to speak of. You whinge and whine in every breath. Nothing is ever good enough for you. You think I'm going to ever come back?

Blast you! That is enough!!

Yes, Stan. That is enough. I've done my time. You were dead long before they put you in the wheelchair. All that's left is to arrange a funeral when the breathing stops.

Get out!!

I'm going, Stan. There's your lunch still warm at the table. I'll leave the keys on the side table. And you can call community services to fill in till you organise my replacement.

Get out!!

Goodbye, Stan. I'm sorry you refuse to give yourself a chance to be happy.

Get out!!

Goodbye, Stan.

61

A dog walks into
a bar - 2

A dog walks into a bar and finds a seat next to a pig.

They are both midway through their dinners when the dog drops his fork dramatically onto his plate and says: "That's it. I can't take it anymore. Why do you do that?"

The pig looks up. "Are you talking to me?"

"Yes," says the dog.

"Stop doing what?"

"I hear no one else make that low-pitched grunting sound as they eat. Can you stop doing that?"

"Sorry Sir, I was just enjoying my dinner."

"So, can you do that without making disagreeable noises!"

"I'm sorry that you find it offensive. It's just that I am really enjoying this dinner."

The dog bangs his paw on the table.

"It is offensive, and you've got to get it under control!"

"Really?"

"Yes really! Hey, Mr Bartender, can you please get this jerk out of here. I'm trying to eat my dinner in peace!"

The pig pauses and says, "Okay, here's the deal. You stop wagging your tail when you eat, and I'll stop grunting when I eat. How about that?"

62

Light and dark

I have a theory, Maya.

Okay?

You want to hear it?

Joel, you don't start by saying you have a theory and then change the subject! Get on with it!

Okay... here's my theory: All of life is light and dark.

That's not a theory. That's not even a freakin figure of speech.

Why not?

Okay, let's assume that it is some sort of theory. It must still be something you can prove.

I can.

Go on... I know your itching to tell me more.

Okay, here's the proof. Every memory you have of a good time is tinged by some shadow.

Really!! Is that your revelation? How many years did it take for you to come up with what everybody knows already?

Of course, everybody knows that we are not in heaven yet. Everybody agrees that there is nothing perfect here. But my theory is more the fact that when good things happen, the force of evil attends close by. The shadows always attend the light.

I'm not so sure about that. There can be unalloyed joy and bliss.

It's great if we experience those peaks, Maya. But they are always touched by shadow. Pain has a way of narrowing the focus. So does joy and pleasure. So, if we are truly honest, the shadow is always there to counter the light. The night Elena was born... remember the broken headlight and dented bumper when someone backed right into our car in the hospital carpark?

Oh, come on! You want to whinge about some damage to the car the same day our daughter was born?

I'm not whingeing. I'm just making an observation. It does not have to be red letter days. Remember getting lost on the beach after what was a wonderful afternoon?

Oh, that was something!

Remember the night before we headed out on our Disneyland holiday? When Rio... what was he then? Just a two-year old pup. Remember how he ripped apart the blinds in our living room?

Yes, that's true.

And what about the head-on collision that wrecked Stafford's Ute the morning he was to pick us up to drop us to the airport for our New Zealand holiday?

Agree... that was more than a bit unsettling.

Remember the hordes of leeches latching onto our bare legs as we trekked through marvellous, moist deciduous forests?

That I'd rather not remember!

Remember me completely missing the cyclist in my blind spot and knocking him over the very day Dad fulfilled his lifelong dream to visit the holy land?

Oh, yes! This has the makings of a pattern!

Remember the kids knocking over that blue vase we loved so much as they romped around with their cousins?

I know!

Remember Marley's tense standoff with the rest of the family the day we had our first family reunion in years?

That was your fault.

I know it was my fault. But that's not the point. Remember getting locked in Keble Chapel just after soaking in Holman Hunt's wondrous painting, 'The Light of the World'?

That was hilarious... until it started getting dark. I was not looking forward to spending the night in an empty centuries-old chapel!

Remember Earl running a high fever the night of his wedding?

Okay... okay... I get it, light and dark. The proof is there. But what does it matter?

I'm not saying it should matter, Maya. I'm only saying that it's there. It's always there. That shapeless shadow of evil that wants to wound even as we celebrate and rejoice.

So, what was the shadow hovering over us the day we got married?

Uh-oh... am I in trouble now?

63

Trick question

He had prepared for it meticulously. He'd broken down the project into small steps. Mapped out the timeframe. Discussed and agreed on the changes that he and his wife would need to make. Sifted the 'wants' from the 'needs' and ruthlessly cut back on the 'wants'. Saved aggressively. Diversified their investments, so that there would be no unpleasant surprises on the homestretch. Paid down the house. Killed the credit cards. Cleared the car loans. Reached zero debt.

And then it happened.

It was just another Wednesday. Nothing special.

Without fanfare, he told his wife that the numbers now stacked up. He was ready to punch out and break free.

They celebrated at the kitchen table with some old wine that was kept aside for this day.

He typed out his resignation email, hit the 'send' and sat back to let it sink in.

That weekend, at his mother-in-law's birthday party, he laughed it off the first time. Laughed a little louder the second time. Sniggered with the others the third time. Ignored the question the fifth time. And simply walked off the tenth time.

"So, what does it feel like," they all asked, "waking up in the morning and having nothing to do?"

64

On the local news

In other news today, a two-year old toddler was killed by a reversing car on the driveway outside her home on Grey's Street, Spring Hill, just before 5.30 pm on Saturday.

Oh, my Lord! Listen to this, Mum.

In what can only be described as extremely tragic circumstances, the driver of the car – the child's father – had assumed that his daughter was in the house as he backed out.

Oh Gosh! How horrible!

Neighbours rushed to the scene, but paramedics could do little when they arrived.

What was that man thinking! Was he on his phone when he backed out?

Treated for shock, the father told police attending the scene that he did not see his daughter in the rear-view mirror as she was down on all fours on their driveway.

Where was the mother in all this?

That's just what I was thinking.

Devastated by the accident, the community of Spring Hill has rallied around the grieving family, even as the coroner prepares his report.

Food's getting cold. Let's eat.

65

A patch of green

Mrs Brent shared a small strip of green with her neighbour, Mr Muneem.

Both were past seventy. Both had buried their spouses. Both received few visitors.

One morning, as Mrs Brent was sweeping away the leaves off her front porch, Mr Muneem came round for a chat.

"Hullo Mrs Brent. Another fine day."

"Morning Mr Muneem. Yes. Another good day."

"I was meaning to ask you something."

"Sure, Mr Muneem. What is it?"

"You know that strip of green between our driveways?"

"Yes" and Mrs Brent looked in the direction of the narrow strip of green.

"I know you've tried your best to get some flowers growing on that strip."

"Yes, Mr Muneem. It's a mystery why I've just not been

able to get anything going on that silly strip. Believe me, I've tried."

"I know you have. I know you have. I was just wondering if I could have a go instead."

"You mean plant something else, and see?"

"Yes, but only if you don't mind."

"Oh, goodness! Why would I mind? Certainly, Mr Muneem, the patch is all yours. Go for it."

Mr Muneem seemed relieved that his suggestion was not taken amiss.

That very afternoon, Mrs Brent looked out of her window to see Mr Muneem vigorously digging out the little that remained of her early efforts. And the next day, she found that he had topped the soil after having planted new saplings – a few flowering plants and some hardy, low-maintenance leafy varieties.

Each time she walked past her driveway to the shops, the park, the clinic, or the church, she glanced at the strip of green that was receiving Mr Muneem's unwavering attention. To her great distress, the plants were flourishing like there was no tomorrow.

One evening as she returned home, she spotted Mr Muneem looking with much pride at the work of his hands. He saw her walking up her driveway and meant to come over and say something, but she hurried in without looking in his direction.

The next day she saw him discussing animatedly with Mr Freeman who had come over from across the street to compliment him on the fine patch of green that he had nurtured with such success.

That afternoon, Mrs Brent saw Mr Muneem lock up and head over to the supermarkets for his weekly shop.

She hurried over to her kitchen, mixed white vinegar with salt and liquid dish soap... poured her concoction into a water spray bottle that she was using for her indoor plants, and headed out to her driveway.

The street was deserted.

Mrs Brent ambled over to the blooms and the leafy greens that were now Mr Muneem's pride and joy. In a matter of minutes, she sprayed her homemade natural weed killer onto every part of the patch.

Making sure that she had emptied the bottle, she went in... made herself a cup of tea... and came out again to sit in the shade of her front porch, exhausted by the flurry of activity. "Too much excitement," she thought, "for one afternoon."

Mrs Brent saw Mr Muneen again only a few days later when she returned from church services. The old man was staring in disbelief at the patch of green, now wilted and dry.

Mrs Brent meant to walk past without saying anything, but then she paused for a bit on the driveway. "Too bad, Mr Muneem. It looks like that patch of green has a mind of its own, doesn't it!"

Mr Muneem merely nodded in defeat.

66

Killing time before the food arrives

Everything is so dense... so "given".

What do you mean?

I mean, we're too lazy to abstract... to distil anymore. Every experience must be pre-packaged and complete. There's no need to stretch... to fill in any gaps... to improvise... to wonder.

So, when did you become the resident philosopher?

I'm serious, mate.

Serious about what?

Serious about the fact that we are distracted and diffused every waking moment. The smartphone owns us. And if it's not something on social media, we are obsessing about our food. Obsessing about our health. Obsessing about people who don't know us. Obsessing about news headlines that don't concern us. We fidget... fuss... and fret. When we do manage to stay still, it's only because we've turned on some tap that fills us with readymade, second-hand experiences. Two hours with a movie. Or ten hours binge watching a TV series. Whole weeks on auto pilot at work. Even holidays – packaged and right-sized so that every box is ticked. I did not sign up for this!

Oh, so you want to walk away from it all, eh? Thoreau at Walden Pond? Get off-the-grid?

That's not what I said. That's probably a cop-out.

Then what do you want to do?

I did not say I know... or that I have the answers!

So rather than make the best of the situation, you choose to whinge?

I'm just saying, we need to wake up from this dream. It may be a comfortable dream. But it's not reality.

And how do you propose to wake up?

I think one way to wake up is to create.

Okay, you did speak highly of "abstraction", but if we want to keep this conversation meaningful, you will have to be more explicit than that. What do you mean, "create"?

I mean, focus on acts of creating rather than acts of consuming.

You mean like your third-rate oil paintings and fifth-rate home video recordings and tenth-rate baking projects?

That's the point. We're too scared about putting out any-thing that does not qualify as first-rate, that we don't commit to anything creative at all.

Okay, so your solution to escaping from zombie land is to "create"?

One of the solutions. I haven't figured it all out, you know.

Okay, so tell me. Once you've painted your oil paintings, edited your home video recordings, and finished off your baking projects, aren't you obsessing about who will buy your paintings, watch your home videos, and give your cakes a "5-stars"?

That's true... it's not always that I can do something just for the enjoyment of it.

Mate, that's my point. You're being too hard on yourself. Down here on this place we call Earth, it's not always easy to get it right every time.

So, what's your suggestion?

Lower your expectations.

That's it?

Mate, take it from me. Your days will be sunnier when you lower the expectations you have of everybody around you and of what you do with yourself.

And why is that?

You will be more thankful, less disappointed, and less wound up.

I'm not wound up.

Knock it off, mate. The food will be here in a minute. Lighten up! Did you watch the game last night?

67

Grade 12 Religion Assignment

In fewer than 600 words, outline the story of Job and discuss what struck you most from it.

There was once a guy in the land of Uz named Job. He had seven sons and three daughters. He was filthy rich. He loved God. But the silly fool had no clue that it was all too beautiful to last.

In some cruel metaphysical joke, Satan wagers with God that Job would not be so holy and spotless if he lost all he had. So, God switches off autopilot and allows Satan to take control.

It does not take long. In one day, Job loses his cattle, his servants, and all his children. And what does Job say? He says, 'Naked I came from my mother's womb, and naked shall

I return there; the Lord gave, and the Lord has taken away; blessed be the name of the Lord.'

So, Satan decides to raise the stakes. He persuades God to let him get physical. And soon, Job is covered in disgusting sores from head to foot. Even his wife tells him to curse God and die. But the fellow is not defeated that easily. His friends come along to gloat. They more than hint that Job got what he deserved. Something along the lines of – 'you do the crime; you do the time'. Job responds by questioning why a just God would crush him so mercilessly.

And then God speaks.

He answers Job out of the whirlwind. 'Where were you when I laid the foundation of the earth?' he asks. And piling it on in language that is breathtaking... unsurpassed, he leaves Job quaking in his sandals. In the end, Job reaffirms his faith in God. And God restores his fortunes. He is blessed with twice as much as he had before and ten children.

He died, old and full of days.

My first observation: I think the poor bloke Job may have been pushed around too much. Some challenge... some pain... I get that. But this fellow was reduced to a freakin shadow. Maybe that was the purpose of the book... to inspire us to find meaning even when the sky falls over our heads. To show us that God is with us in our suffering even if he is silent most of the time. If Job could stay sane in the face of an insane world, we can too.

Second, in all that transcendent poetry, there's not even one specific reason that God gives Job for his suffering. Maybe he does not have to. Maybe, suffering – like all of creation – is not a mystery we mortals can solve. Or maybe, the whole point is that there is such a thing as the innocent having to suffer. Bad things happen to good people. But like Job, we must never lose hope.

Finally, (and this may not be palatable to some) why did it have to be a happy ending? I mean, not everybody's life ends with rewards for being faithful. Of course, what happens to Job at the end was what God had planned for him all along. It wasn't compensation for his suffering. But if Job had to die poor, ill, and alone, would he have stopped cursing the day of his birth and asking 'why?' Who can know?

In summary, it's not a book that's meant to be simplistic and definitive in its answers. There's a lot of counterpoint in this fugue. But much as I admire the man, I just wished the book didn't end as well as it did. Many people never see the light at the end of the tunnel. The writer should have considered that.

68

Love story

Act 1

They were friends first. And then one afternoon, he held her gaze a little longer than usual.

She was troubled by that. And could not sleep at night.

She tried to pay no attention. But like the fragment of a persistent melody, he kept walking into her thoughts uninvited.

Act 2

He looked at her as she slept – tired but radiant – with their two babies.

She had taken his hand, made a home for them and given him two little helpers to light their days.

Act 3

He looked at her as she washed up after dinner.

The two kids had their own kids.

The house was quiet... and empty.

Just the two of them.

She looked worn-out. But she still smiled easily.

Over the years, they had climbed the hills together, hand in hand. And they had learnt to lean into the wind.

Denouement

He looked up as she sat hunched in the chair next to his cold bed.

She still smiled through the grey and the tears.

Someone like her, he thought, made it easy to fight when he felt like fading.

But he knew that he did not have long.

For the last time, he held her gaze a little longer than usual and slipped quietly, gratefully into that good night.

69

Lightning strikes three times

Okay... so it must be something we would never have guessed about you.

Mmm... something you don't know about me?

Yes.

Okay... I'll give you something.

Go on... we're waiting!

Okay... I must have been in my first year of university. I went a whole semester with my right hand in a sling. The unfortunate outcome of a bicycle accident – or so I made the whole campus believe. Thing is, there was nothing wrong with my hand at all!

We don't follow you. You went around with your arm in a sling a whole semester and there was nothing the matter with it?

Yes... nothing at all.

Explain!!

I'm about to. It had to be done. There was no option. Given what happened at the cricket nets at the start of the semester.

What happened?

A few of us boys were at the nets doing some throwdowns for the batsmen in our university team who were prepping for their first game of the season. I was never a certain pick in any cricket team – even the backyard versions as a kid. What I had was a load of good intentions and a love of the game. I could marvel at Tendulkar's cover drive or Warne's leg break. But bat or ball in hand, my contribution was laughable at best.

Of course, no one knew me at the university. So, I quietly shuffled into line to bowl like I belonged.

The guy facing us was a more than competent middle order bloke and he kept smacking our deliveries emphatically. When I say "our", I mean the boys who were in line ahead of me. Our audience was a large number of students who were waiting for us to wrap up before their game of rugby, which was to start on the same ground.

I prayed silently that I would acquit myself reasonably well when it came to my turn. But just before that could happen, the middle order bloke trooped off and in came Dan Towerton, the best batsman in the team! Let me rephrase that – the finest batsman not only in the university, but in the Under-19 state team as well!

The crowd quietened down in anticipation. This short,

right-hand batsman walked into the nets like he owned the place. The two deliveries he faced from my hapless colleague ahead of me were dispatched out of the nets and to the ends of the ground. The sheer mastery of the strokes took the breath away.

It was my turn next.

I've often wondered what it is about fear that changes everything known into the unknown. Going up to my mark, I was not even sure how to grip the ball – Was I going to aim for flat out pace, with index and middle fingers close together at the top of the seam? Or try an inswinger? Or should I be so bold as to try a yorker? What was I thinking! This superstar batsman was going to simply dismember me and stomp on my remains with his metal spiked shoes, while the entire university looked on.

I ran up gingerly.

"Please God, not a mighty six. Just save me now and I will never touch a cricket ball again in my life!"

Dan sized me up with that calm look of a professional executioner.

Somehow, the ball landed on a good length.

Dan made to play a straight drive.

The ball whizzed past and hit the top of off!

I had clean bowled the master!

A ripple went through the crowd. Dan could not believe it. I uttered a limp "Sorry!" as if I had spoiled it all for everybody. Dan paused for a second, bent over, picked up the ball and flung it back at me.

It's alright, I meant to say; I'll just go away quietly.

But Dan was having none of it. I had to bowl again –

just to make it evident that the wicket was nothing more than a fluke.

All eyes were now on me.

I trudged back to my mark, and Dan waited.

This time, I decided to bowl a slower ball.

Dan danced out of his crease, meaning to smack it well over my head and out of the ground. But the ball had other plans and knocked over middle stump.

A loud "Ouch" came from the crowd.

I had bowled Dan Towerton in two consecutive deliveries!

I mumbled another apology. Dan looked at me like I was vermin. I swivelled around and started plodding out of the nets. But Dan scooped the ball up and flung it back at me again. He was not going to let some rookie get away with it.

I muttered aloud, "Last one from me" and went back to my mark.

The murmurs from the crowd grew louder. Someone shouted, "Kill him, Dan!"

I landed the ball short of a good length. Dan was rattled and fended it off just in time to protect his midriff. The ball sailed up and landed softly in my hands. Caught and bowled! A hat-trick against the best batsman around!!

I did not dare glance at Dan. I just walked off into the dazed crowd that parted like I was Curtly Ambrose.

The next day on campus was like one long, surreal victory lap. The oohs and aahs from everyone I met seemed like for another person. Classmates came up to me to find out how I did it... even a couple of professors – who had heard the story – quizzed me about which teams I had played for before.

That afternoon, I bumped into Dan Towerton outside the

cafeteria. He stopped me and muttered quietly, "Come down to the nets this evening... I want to take a closer look at you."

"Sorry, Dan", I mumbled, "Not today... got assignments to catch up on."

"Tomorrow, then."

He walked off without waiting for an answer.

That evening, after a couple of hours at home wondering how I was to extricate myself from certain annihilation the next day, I cycled to the pharmacy and picked up the props I needed.

I mean, what were the chances of me bowling anyone... me bowling Dan Towerton... me taking Dan Towerton's wicket three times in consecutive balls!! No way in hell was I going to muddy the waters.

It was an awfully uncomfortable semester after that. Having to walk around with my perfectly good arm in a sling. But Dan transferred to another university the following semester and I promptly did away with the sling.

To this day, classmates I bump into remind me of that brief but magical spell. I let them roll the superlatives out. Why kill a good story, I say.

70

End of the reign

For the third time, the four cousins came down the path to the clearing and encircled him.

It was not long before the sun would set.

At 14 years, he was already the oldest lion in the pride; battle-hardened, but weaker than the younger males.

The first attack, he managed to out-roar them. But the second attack was serious.

Now, as one of the contenders lunged at him again, he remembered the first time he was near death. He was a little under a year old then, and his mother fought off an intruding male who had taken it upon himself to kill the cub.

As he now parried the fresh blows from the four formidable aggressors, he recalled the first time he was expelled from a pride. That was when he was a three-year-old – a threat to the older pride male. But that time, he had his brothers with him; to help him steer clear of the territories of other prides.

They roamed the savannas then, testing themselves against zebra, buffalo, and larger prey... battling packs of hyenas... till eventually, he won control of his own pride of 12 lions.

That was a long time ago.

Now his dark mane was sparse. His challengers were young, powerfully built, and impatient.

He roared down the two in front of him. But they didn't back down like they did before.

From behind, another pounced on his bleeding back. The fourth grabbed one of his hind legs. He buckled, fell, and rolled over.

Immediately, the two in front attacked his open chest and stomach.

With the weight of four large lions on him, it seemed like he was lost. But summoning the last reserves of strength, he clawed his way back onto his feet, and scattered his rivals.

They were surprised and backed off momentarily.

The old monarch – with blood oozing through his mane and down his back – snarled defiantly. He made to pounce forward, but the deep bite to his spine had done its job and he could only manage a weak flailing of his front paws.

He paused, bowed his head, and panted loudly.

The four foes waited. Swishing their tails, they settled into the dusty ground a few metres away from the king.

The red glow of the fading sun was now right across the dry grasslands. The vultures remained interested.

The old lion let out a guttural rumble. He raised himself up gingerly on his front legs, but something had snapped in his back. Even if he managed to fend off the immediate threat, he was never going to be able to hunt again.

One of the four – sensing that there was not too much more to be done – stood up, took a final look at the vanquished king, and wandered away languidly into the tall grass.

But the other three rose and roared repeatedly as they approached the broken body of their one-time leader.

He roared back and tried to stagger to his feet. But he could not get his hind legs to do his bidding.

They did not hesitate. The largest of the three leapt forward and struck him down with one of his huge front paws. It was a mortal blow, and the old warrior fell back and sideways in a ragged heap.

He lay prone, but still breathing feebly. The victors took turns prodding his limp form. But he could not fight back. He looked up and they could see the fire in his eyes fading slowly.

After waiting with him till it was dark, the three strolled out of the clearing and up the path that led to the waterhole.

Except for his head, the old lion could now not move any part of his body. But his eyes followed them as they disappeared up the path.

He let out a deep, low moan. The fight was ended, but he was still alive.

And then... through the unbearable pain... he heard it.

It was a still night. So, the howling, wailing and the high-pitched cackling of his eternal adversaries – the hyenas – reached him long before the pack had come down the path to the clearing where he lay.

There was a time when he would go out alone to meet them and singlehandedly drive them out of his territory.

But now the old king – knowing full well what was about

to happen – laid his head down, closed his eyes and waited for the final assault.

71

Abeo's first... and last tag

The rest of the guests had left.

Uncle Egbo cleared his throat dramatically and asked me, "So Niko, what do you want to do when you finish school this year?"

"He will go on to law school and become the most famous lawyer in the land," Dad declared with pride.

Uncle Egbo was 18 years older than Dad and was having none of it.

"But Niko, is that what you want to become?"

"No, Uncle. I want to become a graffiti artist."

Dad turned to me. "Iniko, I thought we discussed that. You are too good to waste away on the fringe."

"But Dad, you don't understand. Uncle, please tell him." I was 17 years old, but not beyond pleading with anyone who could help me escape the drudgery of law school.

"So, you want to become the next Banksy, eh?" Uncle Egbo seemed genuinely impressed.

"Egbo, I did not work this hard in this unforgiving country only to see my son fade away in some underground subculture... always on the other side of the law!" Dad was in no mood to reopen a debate I'd been having with him for three years.

"But Niko," Uncle swivelled back to me, "I know you are brilliant at drawing, but surely you aren't considering becoming a vandal... defacing subways and trams?"

"No Uncle!" I came back quickly, so I could set the record straight. "I do not want to be looking over my shoulder the rest of my life. I want to learn and pursue this as a legit profession. They actually pay you these days... they give you paint, and they give you a wall."

Dad shot back, "Where is this coming from? You want to protest? Just choose your cause and sign petitions or go to rallies. Pro-refugee, anti-abortion, anti-war, save the rainforests, save the whales, anti-corruption, pro feminism... take your pick... just don't make it your day job!"

"No Dad, you know I'm not trying to be a brat!"

We couldn't go further. Uncle Egbo was called away, and I was left fuming silently with Dad by my side.

I could sense that he was trying hard to calm himself down before he spoke again.

"Iniko" he said, after a few minutes. "Do you know what your name means?

"No, Dad. You told me, but I don't remember."

"It means 'one who is born during troubled times'."

I remained silent as he continued.

"When we left the war behind and reached this country, your mother and I hoped for better days. But in those years before you were born, it was difficult. Very difficult. This country is wonderful to those who cut themselves to fit the cloth. You have no idea what it took for us to put you through school and get food on the table."

"I'm sorry, Dad." I said. "I know what it cost you. And I don't want to disappoint you."

That was five years ago. I went on to complete law school. And found myself a job at a boutique law firm located a two-hour flight from our city. Dad was happy. So happy that on the night before I was to leave home, he organised a slightly over-the-top party to celebrate. We finished quite late, and Uncle Egbo asked if I could drop him back to his apartment. He walked with a pronounced shuffle and wheezed loudly as I helped him into Dad's old station wagon.

"So, Niko, you made your father happy. You made us all proud."

"Yes, Uncle."

We motored quietly though the dim streets of our suburb for a few more minutes.

"But Niko, are you happy?"

"I suppose so, Uncle. I never did see myself becoming a lawyer, but I took that road. So, it is what it is."

"You are right, Niko. You've always been a sensible boy."

Something in his tone suggested that it wasn't all spoken with approval.

As I drove past the cobbled lane that went under the bridge, Uncle Egbo asked me to pull over.

"But we are still a couple of minutes away from your place."

"I know Niko. But you see that fellow standing on the other side of the road. I'm going to stay here in the car. You go over to him."

"And what Uncle? What is this about?"

"It's my gift to you, Niko. I know you told me that you've never ever tagged a wall. But he is a graffiti artist I've hired for tonight. He has what you need in his bag – spray cans, stencils, gloves... the lot. He's been kind enough to locate for us an unblemished piece of brick wall that you can make your mark on. So go for it!"

"Uncle!"

"Hurry Niko... he's promised to keep a lookout for the cops."

"You shouldn't have!"

"I reckon you have 10 to 20 minutes. It is a deserted spot and its past midnight. But you can't be too careful."

"Why Uncle? Why this? And why now?"

"Niko. I wish you every success in your day job. But a man must have something more to look forward to than his next paycheck. I know you will find your bliss. Eventually. But sometimes, you can go too far down the road to retrace your steps. Your father does not know that I organised this little detour. But I just wanted you to have a go. Just once. Tomorrow you will find your way in another city. But that is tomorrow."

I mumbled a clumsy 'thank you', got out of the car and hurried over to my hired mentor and the blank wall.

In a wild 20-minute burst, I spray, brushed, and stencilled a cacophony of planets, angels, vamps, goblins, birds, and beasts on that wall. My new graffiti artist friend stood watch for any vigilante passers-by.

"You've got talent," he murmured.

"Thanks," I said as I stood back to admire my impromptu effort.

"Don't forget to tag your work."

So, I signed at the bottom.

"What does that say? I thought your uncle said you were 'Iniko'?

"Yes, I am Iniko. But I've signed 'Abeo'. It's the name my uncle suggested to my father when he was thinking up names for me when I was born. My father thought it to be a girl's name... so he stuck with his choice, Iniko."

"So, what does Abeo mean?"

"Abeo? It means 'the bringer of happiness'."

The next morning, on my way to the airport, I asked the cab driver to slow down as we drove past the cobbled lane that went under the bridge.

It looked better in the morning light.

About the Author

Ivan Fernandez's first book - *How Art Can Change Your Life: Life Lessons from Artists Past and Present* - drew insights from painting, music, literature, architecture, sculpture, photography, and films to reaffirm the redemptive nature of art.
A die-hard classical music fan, Ivan plays the violin, paints, and writes short fiction.
An industry research consultant by profession, he lives in Sydney, Australia, with his wife, Marion and their two children, Raphael and Olivia, and their Labrador, Rio.